COME AND HAVE A GO IF YOU THINK YOU'RE COOL ENOUGH!

D1392412

Are you COOL enough to collect the series?

COME AND HAVE A GO IF YOU THINK YOU'RE SMART ENOUGH!

COME AND HAVE A GO IF YOU THINK YOU'RE COOL ENOUGH!

COME AND HAVE A GO IF YOU THINK YOU'RE MAD ENOUGH!

COME AND HAVE A GO IF YOU THINK YOU'RE RICH ENOUGH!

COME AND HAVE A GO IF YOU THINK YOU'RE COOL ENOUGH!

Haydn Middleton

Hippo

Scholastic Children's Books,
Commonwealth House, 1–19 New Oxford Street,
London, WC1A 1NU, UK
a division of Scholastic Ltd
London ~ New York ~ Toronto ~ Sydney ~ Auckland
Mexico City ~ New Delhi ~ Hong Kong

First published in the UK by Scholastic Ltd, 1999

ISBN 0 439 01081 0

Typeset by DP Photosetting, Aylesbury, Bucks
Printed and bound by Bath Press, Bath

1 2 3 4 5 6 7 8 9 10

For Andrew and Calum – Chuck those Celtic shirts and get *blue* hoops!

2

1

The bell went and a small cheer filled the classroom. French was over for another Wednesday morning. Luke Green shut his book, packed his bag and jostled out into the corridor.

Everyone else turned left to trudge off to the gym for double PE. But Luke went right and headed for the main entrance. Through the big glass doors he could already see the taxi waiting. *Honk if you support the Albion!* said a sticker on its back windscreen. With a grin as wide as Wembley, Luke broke into a trot.

"You there – *walk*!" the head barked from her office doorway. "You're not on the pitch yet, you know." Luke hit a lower gear, then glanced at her before opening the entrance door. "And make sure you're back for lunch by twelve," she said, tapping her watch. "On the dot."

"I will be, Miss," Luke said. "Thanks, Miss." Three bags full Miss, he thought as he piled into the back of the taxi. But he couldn't really knock her. Not many heads would let you bunk off school once a week to go to a Nationwide League team's ground. Luckily she was a Castle Albion season-ticket holder herself.

"Ash Acre stadium, then?" said the taxi driver, looking in his rear-view mirror. Luke nodded. He still had to pinch himself to believe it. Ash Acre stadium. Home of his beloved Castle Albion FC. And he was on his way to first-team training. But that was just for starters. On Saturday afternoon he was going to be *playing* – in the FA Cup Fourth Round!

"I saw that Third Round game on the telly," the driver said as they set off through the mid-morning traffic. "You played a right blinder, lad. Before you came on, we wouldn't have won a raffle. You made all the difference."

"Thanks," said Luke. "But there were eleven players out there." That was what they always said in post-match interviews on *Match of the Day*. "It was a good all-round team perfor-mance."

"Don't give me that!" the driver laughed. "I wouldn't let some of those others play in my back garden. It was all down to *you*, lad."

Luke was getting used to this. Two weeks after the historic Third Round win over Aston Villa, everyone from John Motson to the school lollipop lady was still talking about his five-star display. His feet had hardly touched the ground since his team-mates hoisted him shoulder-high at the final whistle.

"I reckon we'll get a result on Saturday too," the driver went on. "As long as *you're* on from the start. No more of this coming-on-as-a-sub business."

"Hmmm," said Luke, grinning out at the banked-up snow on the pavements. "We've just got to take each game as it comes."

But just thinking about the Fourth Round tie was making his toes tingle. Albion of the Third Division had drawn First Division Wolves – away. The game would be played at Molineux, that fabulous footballing Mecca of the Midlands. Luke had only ever seen pictures of Wolves' state-of-the-art ground. But with its undersoil heating he knew there was no chance of the game being snowed off – unlike Albion's last three League matches.

"It's a shame about this lay-off," said the driver as Ash Acre's rickety-looking floodlight pylons came into view at the top of the hill. "We could have done with some League points, couldn't we? What are we now? Nineteenth?"

"Something like that," replied Luke. In fact it was twentieth. Barnet had won at Leyton Orient the night before and had leap-frogged the Albion.

"It seems crazy to me that you can beat Aston

Villa but get turned over by the likes of Mansfield and Rochdale."

"Hmmm," Luke said. "Funny game, football."

"You can say that again." The driver swung the taxi into Ash Acre's car park. "Especially when this bunch of jokers are playing it."

He drew up near the club offices then twisted around in his seat. "Seriously though, lad, you've got to get that defence sorted."

People kept talking to Luke like this too: as if he wasn't just the youngest midfield maestro in the history of British football, but also picked the Albion team and decided all the tactics.

"There's a couple of blokes that just don't cut it. And the worst one of the lot is..." The driver broke off to glance left and right, in case the bloke in question was listening, even though the car park was empty and the car's windows were all wound up. "*Chopper Foggon!*"

"Hmmm," said Luke one more time. There really wasn't any other answer.

"I mean, Chopper's hard. That's for sure. He puts the wind up people. He puts the wind up *me* – and I'm only standing on the terraces. But as for ball skills, he couldn't trap a bag of cement. And he's so slow now he can't run a bath. You tell your Boss from me, lad," he whispered: "*Axe the Chopper!*"

Luke smiled politely, got out and offered him two pound coins. He had to pay for the ride then claim the fare back from manager Benny Webb.

"Keep your money," the driver said. "This one's on me. Just do it for us again on Saturday, right?"

"I'll certainly give it a go," beamed Luke, trotting off.

Wolverhampton Wanderers, he thought as an old guy in an Albion blazer waved him through the players' entrance. *At Molineux. YESSSS!*

2

They call Old Trafford the Theatre of Dreams. At Ash Acre it was more like dozing off and waking up in the middle of a nightmare. The crumbling ground still only had seating on one side. There was so much undergrowth on the terraces that David Attenborough could have made a wildlife documentary. And you didn't even want to think about using the men's toilets. But every time Luke entered this seedy old arena, his heart beat a little bit faster.

Proudly he strode through the peeling corridors towards the home dressing-room. The noise from inside was awesome. Screaming and whooping that would have put his class at school in detention for a week. As Luke came closer, he watched a huge, overripe piece of fruit hurtle through the air, followed by an ear-piercing yell that sounded like Mick Hucknall on helium.

He smiled. This was striker Carl Davey's peculiar ritual. During the lead-up to a big game, the more times full-back Craig Edwards smashed Carl on the bottom with a pineapple, the more likely he was to score. Or so he said.

In the uproar no one noticed Luke come in. Most of the players were watching Madman Mort. Albion's first-choice goalie was up on the physio's bench, giving one of his many impersonations of Aircraft Through The Ages. From the sound of it, this was his "Red Arrow with failing engine". Suddenly from the cockpit he caught sight of the new arrival. *"Is it a bird?"* he hollered, pointing down at Luke.

The others all turned, saw, and chanted back in a chorus: *"No!"*

"Is it a plane?" Madman roared, throwing out his arms and pretending to glide.

"No!"

Again Madman stabbed a finger at the boy in the doorway. *"Then what the heck is it?"*

"It's the Studless Sensation!"

Luke grinned and went over to his peg, getting his hair ruffled by everyone he passed. "Studless Sensation" was what the *Daily Mail* had called him after his debut at Hartlepool three weeks before. He had played in his trainers because his football-hating mum had never let him have a pair of boots. Then he'd masterminded Villa's downfall in a pair of Reebok-lookalikes as well.

"Get changed quick now, son," said Benny

Webb, Albion's big sheepskin-coated manager. "We're having a stiff session this morning. We've got to be at our absolute peak if we don't want to get stuffed by the Wolves." Then he clapped his hands, threw back his bearded head and howled (a bit like a wolf in sheepskin-clothing himself) for some hush from all the others.

"Now then, now then," he said when everything had quietened down. "It's chaos in here. And you're all very full of yourselves today. But you've always got to remember this: in football you're only as good as your last game."

He paused to let that sink in. "But we won that one, Boss," skipper Stuart "Gaffer" Mann quietly reminded him. "Villa. Three-one." Everyone cheered loudly.

"You know what I mean," Benny grunted.

"The last game but one?" Dennis Meldrum helpfully suggested.

"No, that was Hartlepool away," put in Chrissie Pick, a YTS lad who had just broken into the first team – and the proud owner of The Biggest Hair In The Nationwide League. "We won there as well. Two-one." Another whopping cheer.

"The game before that then?" Carl Davey asked, still rubbing his bottom from where the pineapple had hit. "Southend at home. We went down one-three."

Above a round of boos and hisses, Carl nodded smugly at the pineapple between his feet. "I did score our solitary goal though." At that, the dressing room was flooded by a wave of catcalls and abuse even filthier than the away-end toilets.

"Shut it! Shut it! Shut it!" moaned Benny Webb, waving his arms about in frustration. "You *know* what I'm saying here. None of you can afford to take anything for granted. You'll *all* have to play out of your skins at Molineux. And the Cup is just the icing on the cake. Our bread-and-butter is the League and there's a long hard struggle ahead there, I can tell you."

He paused to squint up at Madman Mort, still on the physio's bench and doing one of his quieter airborne impressions: Richard Branson's balloon in free fall. "*You*," Benny rasped. "What have I just been saying?"

Continuing to "float", and with his eyes shut tight, Madman answered in a dreamy voice: "That we're only as good as our last game but two, Boss. And that the Cup is the icing on our bread-and-butter."

"Spot on," Benny snorted. "And I hope that's clear to all the rest of you too. Now let's get out on the pitch and pick up again where we left off."

Bawling again, the players rushed out in their bibs and leggings. Madman leapt off the bench on to the back of Trinidadian international Narris Phiz, and rode him all the way out to the pitch, tilting his arm in front of his nose and pretending to be Concorde. Luke finished changing and ran up the tunnel last of all.

Benny was standing at the edge of the pitch, looking up at the nest of black redstarts in the stand's roof. "Luke," he said, waving him over. "D'you reckon that mate of yours is going to turn up? You know – Frederick, the boy who don't say much? I couldn't give him his trial two weeks ago because of all the snow. So I rang and left a message with his sister, asking him to come and train with us today. D'you think he's still interested?"

"Why don't you ask him yourself?" grinned Luke, pointing.

Benny turned to watch a boy of Luke's age stroll up the tunnel, finishing a call on a mobile phone. His name was Dulac, Frederick Dulac – one part Rio Ferdinand to two parts Calvin Klein. Was he cool? Was snow white? This kid was so laid-back he was almost horizontal. And when he came into the empty stadium, taking a good long look all around him, Luke suddenly thought he heard a capacity crowd roaring back in salute. Cool Frederick just had that sort of effect. Stepping out on to the pitch, he nodded first at his good friend Luke, and then at Benny Webb. "Respect," he breathed.

3

Benny didn't introduce the newcomer to the rest of the squad. Most of them had met him already. Frederick had travelled up to the Hartlepool game as Luke's guest. Then at a service-station kick around on the way home, he had shown so much skill that Benny had invited him for a trial. This, at last, was it.

The manager had promised a stiff session and he wasn't kidding. Since this was the first time they had trained on grass for two weeks, Benny made sure everyone remembered what it tasted like: hundreds of press-ups, dozens of wheelbarrow races, lots of sheer flat-out gasping for breath. "Can't we practise diving in the penalty area now?" panted midfielder Michael "Half-Fat" Milkes.

"You keep working, Milkesey, and get some of that weight off," Benny shouted back. "I don't know about 'Half Fat'. From where I'm standing you look more like Full Fat with Extra Cream."

"Oh do behave, Boss," Dennis Meldrum

pleaded. "Can't we do something with a *ball*? We're gonna forget what it looks like, come Saturday."

"OK then, Dennis, just for you." The manager tossed a ball into the full-back's arms. "Run round the pitch ten times holding that in front of you."

But after another fifteen minutes of back-breaking exercises, Benny got everyone together and picked two sides for a practice match – with work experience lads making up the numbers. He put both Luke and Frederick on Team Two. "You, son," he said to Frederick. "Where do you normally play?"

"In a baby bouncer?" sneered a bullet-headed veteran with tree-trunk thighs, standing apart from everyone else, and with his arms folded. Some of the others tittered. It was usually a good idea to titter at this guy's "jokes". If you didn't, and you got him on a bad day, he had ways of *making* you laugh. For this was Chopper Foggon, Albion's leaky defensive stopper (*motto*: It's Good To Talk, But Better To Bite). Frederick smiled straight back at him and nodded. "Sweeper," he told Benny.

"Well, we're playing with a flat back-four now," Benny said. "You'll have to slot in as a twin centre half alongside Gaffer Mann. Give it your best shot."

The game was pretty messy to start with.

Then Luke threaded a ball past Chopper for Half-Fat to run on to. The midfielder shot first time and Madman tipped it away for a corner. Gaffer Mann waved Frederick up for the set piece, which Luke ran across to take. While he was placing the ball he saw Chopper jostling his mate on the goal-line. Just his usual week-in, week-out stuff: an elbow here, a shirt-tug there. Frederick took it all in his stride and as soon as Luke started his run-up, he ghosted out towards him.

Luke understood. They had practised this move over and over in the park. He had to drop his corner just inside the six-yard box. Then Frederick would hook it back over his own head and into the goal. Luke flighted the ball in, but just as Frederick went for it, Chopper clipped his heels. Down went Luke's mate – but, with breathtaking agility, he sprang up again to meet the cross on the volley and caress it into the net at Madman's near post. One-nil to Team Two.

Chopper didn't look best pleased as Frederick was mobbed and the game restarted. And he didn't get much happier over the next half an hour. His side spent most of the time encamped in Team Two's half, so he couldn't get much chopping in. All he *could* do – along with everyone else – was admire the silky defensive skills of the new schoolboy trialist.

There were no two ways about it, this kid was

tasty. He was shadowing ex-West Brom, Chelsea and Tottenham striker Ruel Bibbo – once one of the first black players to be capped by England. But however many balls were lofted or driven into Team Two's box, Frederick always got there first. By the time Ruel pulled up short with his regular groin-strain and went off for treatment, he hadn't had a single shot.

With fewer defensive duties, Frederick began to link smoothly with Luke in midfield. The two boys' interpassing was different class. In one zigzagging move they cut Team One to shreds – and put Half-Fat clean through on goal again. Chopper wasn't having any of that. Puffing along in the midfielder's wake, he shot out a leg and scythed him down. Penalty.

Craig Edwards stepped up. He hit the kick hard and well to Madman's left. But the keeper spread himself brilliantly and fisted it away. Then he raced to the North Stand to receive fanatical acclaim from all the empty seats. Benny had seen enough. He blew the final whistle: "Last one in the bath likes Chelsea!"

As the players trooped off, no one passed Frederick and Luke without a good-natured wind-up: "You won't be too bad when you grow up, son." "Where'd you learn those moves – *Blue Peter*?" Only Chopper stomped by in silence. Even his beads of sweat looked stroppy.

"Well, lads," said Benny Webb, putting a hand on each boy's shoulder and walking off with them. "That was some exhibition. I'd definitely like to sign you up too, Frederick. You live with your big sister, right? I'll need her signature as your guardian on the signing-on forms. Could I come round tonight?"

"Rockin'," purred Frederick.

"Smashing. And I'd like you to travel with us to Wolves on Saturday. I'm not going to change a winning team, but I'll put you on the bench – just in case."

"Safe."

"And you, Luke? You're all right for getting to Molineux?"

"It's all sorted, Boss." Luke's football-hating mum still didn't know he was playing for Albion. If she ever found out she would throw such a wobbler that even Chopper Foggon would sit and take notes. So Luke needed the menfolk in his family to cover for his match-day absences. "My stepdad told my mum he's taking me to a conference on Orni-Ornithi-Orno..."

"Ornithology," said Frederick, who was *well* clever – although he showed up for fewer school lessons per week than Bobby Charlton had hairs on his head.

"That's it. All about birds."

"Well make sure you're there in good time,"

said Benny as they came off the pitch. Then he glanced sideways and shook his head in disbelief. Madman was *still* doing a victory jig in front of the North Stand to celebrate his penalty save. "Just between you and me," he said, "I sometimes wonder if he needs help."

It was embarrassing. Deeply embarrassing. But Luke depended too much on his stepdad Rodney to kick up a fuss. He would just have to grin and bear it...

They had reached Wolverhampton in good time and after parking the 1978 Escort in a narrow street of terraced houses, the mad-keen ornithologist was kitting himself out for the game. To hoodwink Luke's mum, he had left home in his usual bird-spotting outfit: puffer jacket, old jeans, green wellies, binoculars around his neck. But now that he was safely out of her sight, he pulled on something else. Normal Albion supporters decked themselves out in blue-and-white hooped shirts, scarves and hats. With Rodney it was a frilly pink pinny.

Luke looked away as he tied a big bow. He had been wearing this pinny to wash up after lunch at the start of Albion's televised Third Round game. Albion had run out three-one winners; and to Rodney's warped way of thinking, the pink pinny had helped to make it happen. So he'd vowed to wear the thing at every game until Albion were knocked out of the FA Cup – or perhaps until he was knocked out himself. From the looks on some of the passing Wolves fans' faces, Luke wondered if he was going to reach the ground in one piece.

They set off through the slush at a brisk pace. There was over an hour till kick-off but the roads to Molineux were already chock-a-block. This was serious football country. These people in black and gold were walking serious football walks. Wolves might no longer have been the global football force of old. But every Wolves fan from pensioner to babe-in-arms still thought they should be.

Here was a club that had once been League champions three times in six years. They had won the FA Cup *four* times. And their legendary heroes were as big as they came: Billy Wright, Tim Flowers' dad Ron, Derek Dougan, Andy Gray who now did the *Sky* commentaries – and last but not least, the veteran ex-England goal-machine who would be lining up against Albion today, "Tipton Terror" Steve Bull. Chopper Foggon was going to have his work cut out there.

As the futuristic-looking ground loomed up ahead, fewer people stared at pink-pinnied Rodney and more at the boy by his side. When

Luke stopped to buy a programme, he found out why. On the pages headed *Today's Visitors* there was a special box marked *One to Watch*. Inside was a cracking action pic of Luke leaving Gareth Southgate for dead in the Villa game, with the caption:

This boy has it all in front of him. At the end of the day it's all about taking your chance when it comes, and Luke Green has taken his in both hands – and both studless feet. From a Wolves' point of view, let's hope he slips up today!

"Luke!" came a voice from near the main entrance. "Here, mate!"

Luke looked up to find Terry Vaudeville, the Albion physio, waving from a doorway. "Come and get changed, son," he shouted. "We're all in here."

After saying goodbye to Rodney (and wondering if he really *ought* to advise him against the pinny) Luke needed a reality check. It was so plush inside Molineux, he could hardly believe the place was meant for football. He found the rest of the Albion team wandering round the dressing room looking shell-shocked too. "I'm not sure I like this," said a strangely subdued Madman. "I can't smell ghastly-burgers. And the tannoy system actually works!"

"Go out and have your warm-up now, lads," said Benny Webb. Even he had a funny glint in his eye. Perhaps he'd been inspired by the fabulous atmosphere. Or maybe, like half the rest of them, he was just scared witless.

The ground looked jam-packed already. Luke gazed up in awe at the soaring stands on all four sides, then down in amazement at the lushness of the midwinter turf.

"Come On You Wo-olves!" rang out at deafening volume across the pitch.

Then a ball rolled against Luke's ankle like a cat asking to be stroked. Luke looked round. Frederick in his sub's tracksuit had played it to him. Now with a grin he wanted it back. Pre-match nerves for the new boy? *As if!* To Frederick this was just another park kick-around. They got straight into a regular passing rhythm. And pretty soon Luke forgot about every single thing except the need to play out of his skin and do the business once the whistle went.

But when they went back inside for Benny's team talk, some of the others were still not on song. Craig Edwards' pineapple-shot at Carl Davey's bottom was a bit limp. Even Ruel Bibbo – who had seen all this before and bought the T-shirt – sat rubbing his dodgy groin and didn't seem up for it.

"OK then," Benny began, sweltering in his sheepskin under the heaters, "I'll keep this brief. This lot might be two divisions higher than you, but the Cup is a great leveller. And this, today, is what football is all about. The fat cats against the game's poor relations. The haves against the have-nots. You all know what you've got to do. Not just for us but for every club *like* us." He narrowed his eyes and his voice rose with passion. *"If the dream of the small club dies, then the soul of this game goes with it!"*

And that was it.

In an eerie silence Gaffer looked at Half-Fat who glanced across at Narris Phiz who frowned at Dennis Meldrum. There had been no "You tuck in, Craig," or "Keep pushing up, Luke," or "No soft corners, Chopper." Nothing on the Need For Smart Football or the Element Of Surprise. Benny had said his bit. And only Frederick was nodding his head. All the other players' eyes were drawn to him.

"Cool," the sub finally said.

"Yeah – cool!" echoed Carl Davey after a short pause. "Cool!" yelled Half-Fat, punching the air. Then they were all on their feet, punching, whooping, stamping – and in Madman's case, being a World War Two Junkers Ju 87B dive-bomber.

"Now get out there," Benny Webb's emotionally-charged voice blared above them all, "and do it for yourselves. Do it for me. Do it for the fans. And do it for the Nationwide League Division Three!"

Fifteen minutes later Albion were a goal behind. In all fairness it could have been three. On the one hand they'd completely frozen on the big occasion. On the other they were charging about like headless chickens. Frozen headless chickens, then. Not a pretty sight for the 2,200 travelling Albion faithful who were shielding their eyes behind the Wolves goal.

Chopper Foggon was suicidally at fault for the goal. Simon Osborn, Wolves' little midfield wizard, chipped a delicate through-ball up to Steve Bull. Its flight so bewitched Pick and Phiz that they ran into each other and missed it altogether. The rampaging Bull touched it on, turned and raced for goal. There was no immediate danger. Mann and Meldrum were covering the angles closer to goal. But Chopper had a rush of blood and went for Bully.

"Here Comes The Chopper!"
bellowed the Albion fans, more in alarm than hope, as they watched their big bad

stopper start his slide-tackle from ten yards away.

Maradona called it the Hand of God when he palmed in his goal against England. Now this – courtesy of Chopper Foggon – was the Foot Of Satan.

"To Chop Off Your Legs!"

the fans continued. Then they joined in the stadium-wide gasp and wince as contact was made.

Luckily Bully had good peripheral vision. He caught a glimpse of the knee-high boot coming at him like a shark's fin – and sprang into the air, so Chopper only caught his ankle. But still he went sprawling. And immediately half a dozen furious Wolves' players rushed at the ref to get him to red-card the hard man.

Chopper got up grinning, but not for long. The ref was already putting pencil to paper and he wasn't making a shopping list. He reached into his back pocket for a card – and all but 2,200 people in the ground bayed in disgust when it turned out to be only yellow. Again Chopper grinned.

"Here Comes The Chopper!"

the Albion fans chanted a second time, sounding relieved but even less convinced than before. Then came the real punishment.

The ref gave a direct free kick from where the attempted assault had taken place. Twenty-five yards out from goal, maybe even thirty. At once Chopper, shoving and pointing and screaming blue murder, set about organizing a wall.

It takes all sorts of players to make a football world. Some like scoring goals, some get their kicks from stopping them, others find true beauty in perfectly-worked set-pieces. But with Chopper Foggon nothing on God's earth could beat building a defensive wall. This was where his full footballing genius could come into play. This was what he was *for*.

Getting more and more frenzied, he dragged a player out here, pressed another one in there. If he'd had his way, he would have stuck Bibbo, Phiz, Milkes and Edwards together with real cement, then put a line of barbed wire and broken glass along their heads. But when the ref blew his whistle and Simon Osborn shaped up for his shot, reluctantly the Chopper had to down tools.

Linking arms with Ruel Bibbo, cupping his hands over his privates, he glared with spine-chilling menace at the kicker, daring him to find a way through.

Osborn didn't even bother to look for a gap. Instead he saw that Chopper himself, ignoring Madman's shrieks, had closed up too tight on Ruel and left a yard or so of the net exposed. Three seconds later the ball was nestling in the back of it. One-nil. The noise the Wolves fans made wasn't good. It wasn't good at all. But it was a whole lot better than the look on Chopper's face.

Now that they were chasing the game, Luke tried to warm up Albion's play a bit. It was time, he decided, to put some heads on the chickens. Dropping deeper, he won more of the ball, then sprayed around a stunning array of passes. Twice he sliced the Wolves defence apart with laser-sharp through-balls. But no one else in the team could thaw out enough to make use of them.

In between times, Bully and Co were blasting shots at Madman for fun. It was a miracle that there was still only one goal in it. And because Luke was tearing about trying to do so much, he skidded over a few times on the greasy surface. Even designer-grass like Molineux's wasn't meant to be played on in trainers in the middle of winter.

Benny had his face to the wall when the Albion lads trooped into the dressing room at half-time. No one spoke as they sat and waited for another roasting. "*What ... was ... that?*" Benny hissed in the end, still facing the clothes-pegs. "*What game were you lot playing out there? 'Cos it wasn't football!*"

Then he turned around and he looked as if he'd been crying. His teeth were gritted, and he was glaring madly at the trayful of sugared teas on the table. Luke was mighty glad Benny didn't belong to the school of half-time teacup-throwers. Someone like Alex Ferguson would have been knee-deep in shattered crockery by now.

From Craig Edwards right round to Cool Frederick, everyone braced themselves for a tongue-lashing. But it didn't come. The silence lengthened, deepened, got more and more uncomfortable. Luke and Frederick swapped baffled glances. Narris Phiz chewed his lip. Dennis Meldrum cleared his throat. It was like being in a graveyard. A cemetery for headless chickens.

On and on went the waiting until finally Benny opened his mouth. "*That*," he said, "is what it'll be like on the coach all the way home if you don't get yourselves sorted. And *that*'s what it'll be like for those 2,200 poor saps stuck up there behind the goal supporting you. Do you *want* that? Do you *want* a silent, shameful journey home for everyone connected with this club?"

There was an intake of breath all round. Then it began. "No, Boss," muttered Craig Edwards, shaking his head. "No, Boss," said Half-Fat Milkes, a bit more defiantly. "No, Boss," growled Gaffer Mann, oozing new determination. "No, Boss," Madman chimed in, working

27

up to his usual volume. "No way, Boss," Cool Frederick added. And soon the whole dressing room was shaking to the sound of "*No, No, No, No, NO!*"

"Then get back out there!" Benny roared, pointing at the door. "And do what you know you've got to do!"

Good psychology, thought Luke as he leaped up and joined the hollering stampede. The Element Of Surprise. You had to hand it to old Benny Webb sometimes. After an off-the-wall rollicking like that, things just had to get better. They couldn't get any worse. *Could* they?

Four minutes into the second half Chopper gave away a penalty. A fairly aimless Wolves cross floated into the Albion area. Chopper rose unchallenged like a middle-aged salmon, flicked his neck for a clearing header – and met the ball smack on the palm of his hand.

It was a second bookable offence but for some reason the ref didn't send the culprit for an early bath. 25,000 Wolves fans seemed a little bit upset by that. But they still had their penalty. Deadly Steve Bull put the ball on the spot.

Now Luke wasn't sure if he believed in *déjà vu*. He wasn't even sure he knew what it meant. Something to do with thinking you've lived through an incident before? Anyway, for the next two seconds he was convinced that he'd seen all *this* before. Only last Wednesday morning. In training.

Bull charged in and planted his kick just where Craig Edwards had aimed his shot for

Team Two. Madman took off and spread himself in just the same way. Fist met ball. Ball veered off out of harm's way beyond post. Penalty saved! The only difference from Wednesday was that halfway into his celebratory charge towards the stand on his left, Madman realized that *here* the cheering Albion faithful were all behind his goal. Swivelling around, he milked the wild applause. Then he was swamped by ten extremely relieved team-mates.

That should have been the turning-point. With Luke pulling the strings from midfield, Albion danced their way back into the game. Ruel fired just wide in front of a gaping net. Narris hit a post from three feet. Sooner or later someone *had* to score. But with Chopper still on the pitch, it was just as likely to be Wolves. Every time the home team broke, he looked like shipping a goal.

Then with twenty minutes left there was an incident that Luke had *never* seen before. Chopper went for a tackle near the Albion dugout. He missed the ball, clattered his man, and stayed down pretending to be injured himself. So far, this was pretty much par for the course. Chopper liked a mid-match breather.

On came the stretcher, off went the play-actor. **"There GOES The Chopper!"** sang the Albion fans. They all expected him back after a swig or two from the canister. But no! This time it was different. Quick as a flash Benny decided to play his stopper in a more withdrawn role – withdrawn from the game altogether. Terry the Physio was already holding up two cards. The "six" meant Chopper was off. The "fourteen" meant Cool Frederick was about to make his début.

"There WENT The Chopper!"
came a rather nervous chorus from behind Madman's goal. He jumped up from his stretcher looking as if he'd just been mugged by Father Christmas. Then with a murderous glare at his manager, he turned and stormed off down the tunnel for first go at the soap.

Luke high-fived Frederick for luck as his mate trotted past to plug the massive defensive hole. Even though he was wearing the same kit as everyone else, Frederick somehow looked a whole lot sleeker – as if he had got Giorgio Armani to run him up a special set of shirt, shorts and socks the night before. "O-K," he drawled to Luke. "Let's play some sexy football."

Luke was a bit young to know much about sex. But if it involved stopping Steve Bull from getting another kick all afternoon, then this was sure-fire eighteen-certificate stuff. From the word go Frederick had Bully so deep in his pocket, he must've wondered if he would ever get out again. Yet the super-sub wasn't content with that. Every time he won the ball, he *used* it at once – with control, vision and, above all, coolness. No mindless hoofing here. He turned defence into attack as effortlessly as Chopper's tackles turned fans' stomachs.

With nine minutes left on the clock, he played his best ball yet. A raking thirty-five yarder to Luke, out wide on the right. Deep inside the Wolves half, Luke took it on his thigh, and before it touched the ground, he looped a cross into the box. Ruel was sprinting for the near post, with defender Keith Curle trying to get inside his shirt. But Luke hadn't aimed for the big guy this time. He'd spotted Carl Davey stealing in further back – one step ahead of *his* marker.

One step was all it took. Carl struck his volley from the edge of the six-yard box – not a screamer, just a scrappy sidefoot past the flailing keeper – but it doesn't matter how hard they hit the net. All that mattered was the scores were level!

Carl wheeled away and raced back towards the Albion end. Gleefully he grinned at Craig Edwards and pointed to his bottom. The Albion fans had heard all about his bizarre big-match ritual. Slowly a huge inflatable pineapple rose up above their heads as they broke into:

"One Carl Davey!
There's Only One Carl Davey!"

They were still singing as Frederick intercepted a hit-and-hope long ball straight from the kick-off. Nudging it forward, he feinted past one opponent while two more backed off for fear of being taken out too. On Frederick loped: straight-backed, perfectly balanced, constantly weighing up his options to right and left, and with the ball attached to his boot by invisible elastic.

"Have a pop, son!" yelled Ruel, taking Curle wide on a decoy run as the goal opened up. And with minimal backlift, Frederick did just that. From all of thirty yards he let fly, curling his shot past the keeper's despairing dive. But instead of flying into the net, the ball hit the angle of post and bar, cannoned down on to the keeper's back, then rolled behind for a corner.

As Luke ran over to take it, the fans in black and gold all went very quiet. "The kid's OK," Luke plainly heard Gaffer Mann tell Dennis Meldrum behind him. "Reminds me of Alan Hansen when he used to play with his feet, not his mouth." Luke smiled. He knew it was a case of Wolves to the slaughter now.

Frederick stayed up for the corner. Dean Richards was right behind him but it was still worth a try. Luke dropped in the kick just where Frederick wanted it. Richards moved too late. Frederick didn't. The keeper wasn't just beaten at his near post – he was thrashed within an inch of his life. Albion were ahead!

The fans behind Madman's goal went bananas. And pineapples. Luke even saw a deliriously-bobbing patch of pink amid the sea of blue and white. Frederick glided back to his defensive duties, high-fiving all the way.

The Albion had four minutes to hang on to their lead. The result was never in doubt. Frederick's cool, calm approach seemed to spread throughout the whole team. However much the Wolves huffed and puffed, *this* house wasn't coming down.

At the final whistle Luke jumped a mile. They were in Round Five! Glancing at the tunnel, he saw someone else who found it incredible. Chopper Foggon – up from the bath with a towel around his waist. And boy, did he *not* look chuffed.

7

Sunday was a bit of a come-down after the Wolves wonder-show. Luke's mum was not in a great mood. There was no chance of her finding out about the game from the papers. She always threw away the football pages before reading the rest. But *Gardeners' Get-Together* on TV had been replaced by live coverage of the Fourth Round Cup-tie between Leeds and West Ham. For her, that was like a kid finding Christmas has been replaced by quadruple Geography.

Luke and Rodney tiptoed round the house all morning for fear of setting her off. They ate up all the burnt Tesco's lasagne she served late for lunch and even congratulated her on it afterwards. Then she got a splitting headache. "Why don't you go and lie down?" suggested Luke as he did the drying up.

Crunching aspirins, she eyed him suspiciously. And with good reason. If she went upstairs, Luke planned to watch the Leeds v West

35

Ham second half with the mute button on. Fat chance. She draped herself over the sitting-room sofa, ordering tea and magazines from Rodney. Luke just went and finished off his homework in the dining room. Then quietly he put on an ancient King Crimson CD. His dad, an extremely low-level pop star – in fact more of a small crashed meteorite – had lent it to him to "educate himself".

"Turn that *off*!" his mum roared as the opening notes of "21st Century Schizoid Man" dared to seep through the French doors to where she was suffering. Luke could only obey. But when he sat down again in the dreary silence, Rodney came in with his greasy old Walkman.

"Here you are," he said, handing it over with an odd smile, "you can listen to this, if you like." A whiny voice was coming out of the ear-piece.

"No, that's all right," Luke said, quickly handing it back. His dad's musical taste was weird enough – he'd liked almost *nothing* since the end of the sixties. But Rodney's tastes were something else again. He listened to country-and-western tapes on this thing while he watched jackdaws and swallows – *and* he jigged about to it and sometimes murmured "Eee-haww!" at key moments.

"Take it," he insisted now though. "Listen a minute." Again he grinned strangely, glancing back over his shoulder at Luke's mum who was just within earshot. "I'm *sure* you'll like it." He winked. "Number *fourteen*."

Frowning, Luke fitted the ear-piece. To his surprise – and relief – the whiny voice didn't turn out to be Dolly Parton or Tammy Wynette. It wasn't even female, and it wasn't singing either. Luke met Rodney's eye and suddenly it all made sense. They grinned at each other. His stepdad had switched the Walkman to Radio mode – *Radio Five Live* mode to be precise. It was too late to catch the end of the football commentary. But this was even more interesting. The voice was an FA official's, and he was introducing the draw for the Fifth Round of the Cup!

"Number six," it started. "Port Vale ... will play ... number nine ... Arsenal."

Only Luke could hear it, and even he wasn't hearing properly. He was way too excited. Every time a ball was drawn he prayed for Albion's number to come up. Fourteen, Rodney had said. But time after time, it didn't. And each time Rodney widened his eyes in anticipation, Luke had to quickly shake his head. Man United, Spurs, Stoke, Forest, Chelsea, Ipswich, Wimbledon ... but where on earth were the Albion? Then the moment came:

"Number fourteen..." First out of the hat – they were at home! "...One of this season's giantkillers: Castle Albion..." Gleefully Luke nodded as Rodney's wide eyes asked the question yet again. "Will play ... number eight..." Luke screwed up his whole face as he waited to hear the next name, hardly able to breathe now with excitement. "...Ruud Gullit's Newcastle United!"

"*Yeahhh!*" Luke yelled – for a wild moment forgetting all about his mum and her headache, and leaping up to pummel the air.

"Whatever is *up* with you!" his mum yelled back, with a face as dark as Carl Davey's bruised bottom. Sheepishly Luke pulled out the ear-piece. But before he could even think of an explanation, the phone rang.

"Yes!" hissed his mum, after snatching up the receiver. "Who is this and what do you want?" (When it came to easy-going charm, Des Lynam had nothing on Luke's mum.) Her face creased up, she put a hand to her aching head.

"Let me take it, dear," said Rodney, reaching out. "Don't interrupt your rest."

"No," she grimaced. "It's not for us. It's for *him*!" She glared at Luke, then thrust the receiver towards him.

"Hello?" said Luke, half-turning away as Rodney resettled her on the sofa.

"Luke! It's Dad! Mum's got a headache, right? Hey, fab game yesterday. Caught you on *Match of the Day*. You had a scorcher. Frederick too. Can't leave *him* out now, can they? Old Chopper's for the chop, right? And did you just hear the draw for Round Five? Newcastle at home! Brilliant! You'll only be out there on the same pitch as Alan Shearer! Brilliant or what?"

"Yes," Luke said in a flat voice, trembling from both the excitement and the way his mum was squinting up at him from the sofa. "Brilliant."

"Can't talk 'cos of Mum, eh? I get the picture. No probs. But look, I'm calling to see if I can have you on Thursday evening. Albion are running that Karaoke Fundraiser, right? You'll want to be there. I could take you. Ask your mum."

"Mum," Luke said, turning and steeling himself. "Can I go over to Dad's on Thursday?" He couldn't tell her what for. "Just for a quiet evening in?"

She rolled her eyes as if it was the most outrageous question ever asked in the history of parenting. Still holding her head, she began to shake it. "That'll be all right dear, won't it?" Rodney bravely prompted her. "Just for an hour or two?"

Lip curled, she weighed it up. "If you're not back here by ten o'clock," she hissed, "it's the last time you'll ever go out on a school evening. Now hang that thing up and give me some peace! All I ever get in this house is *noise*!"

"She says it's OK, Dad," Luke whispered, wondering if his mum could see his grin through the back of his head. "I'll see you Thursday."

8

On Wednesday morning Luke skipped out of school for his weekly training session. The taxi was waiting as usual. As usual he rolled up at Ash Acre. But rather *un*usually he found the ground empty of giantkilling footballers, managers and physios.

"Oh, didn't anyone tell you, love?" asked one of the secretaries. "Benny arranged a practice match over at Vista Park – to give the pitch here a rest. Oh dear, what a shame. We can't really run to another taxi-fare, and there's no one left who can drive you. Your best bet would probably be to catch a bus outside."

The bus arrived twenty minutes later. Then there was another long hold-up in town where the traffic-lights had failed. Luke drummed his fingers on the misty back window. Then he drew a little pin-man footballer. Then he carefully wrote *Honk if you support the Albion*, backwards.

He was bored and disappointed to be

spending his best morning of the week like this, but not really surprised. Albion weren't exactly the best-run club in Britain. Other clubs might become PLCs and float themselves on the Stock Market. With Albion, you were lucky if the staff remembered to open up the gates on match days. Over the years it hadn't been a case of Public Limited Company so much as Pretty Laughable Conduct. The ground had gone to ruin, there was never enough cash in the kitty – and the club's official sponsors, a local store called Lampshades Plus, weren't exactly shovelling fresh funds in.

That was why events like Thursday's Karaoke Fundraiser were vital. It would be awful if the Albion's Cup-run took them all the way to Wembley, but then they couldn't afford a coach to get there. How would the TV helicopter show an aerial view of the squad, if they were all rolling up separately in trains and buses and taxis – or quite possibly, in Madman's case, in a hijacked Lear jet?

When he got to Vista Park, Luke had to sign an autograph for a man planting bulbs in the flower beds. "Gonna do Scarborough this Saturday, then?" the old boy asked. Luke smiled. The next League game was a real six-pointer. Scarborough were one of only three teams still below them in the table and Albion had home advantage – whatever that was worth.

"Ah, there you are, son," sighed Benny Webb when Luke ran over. "Been wondering where you'd got to. Get those trainers off and stick these on." He tossed him a crumpled box of brand new Adidas Predator boots. Luke had seen them before. They'd been a gift from one Neil Veal, a very persistent players' agent desperate to add Luke to his roster of clients. Luke's mum hadn't been so keen. First she'd hurled the boots at Veal's head, then she'd thrown them away in the rubbish. Obviously the less glamorous side of agenting nowadays involved rooting around in players' mums' wheelie-bins.

"But I've never played in boots, Boss," Luke reminded his manager. "It'd take me ages to get used to them."

"Well you can start right now," said Benny. "You can't keep slippin' over like you did against Wolves." He was looking at the game in progress, not at the Studless Sensation. At that moment Cool Frederick brought the ball out of defence. When he saw Luke he nodded, and without even looking he nutmegged Narris at the same time. "Go on, son," Benny urged Luke. "*You* don't need match practice. Just put 'em on and walk around a bit."

He broke off to make a flurry of hand signals that no one on the pitch could possibly have understood. Several players stopped and blinked, utterly baffled. Benny was always going on about the Element Of Surprise. One day he'd *really* surprise them all, and make a tactical point that made some sense.

Once Luke had the boots on they didn't feel quite so odd. After a while he even managed to run and turn. Maybe he *could* give them a go on Saturday. After all, if boots had been good enough for Pelé, Johan Cruyff and Ronaldo, who was Luke Green to stay studless?

But after a couple of minutes, he was thinking less about his feet than about one of the players out on the pitch. Mister Chopper Foggon. The practice match was nearly over. In between hand signals, Benny kept looking at his watch and he had the whistle in his mouth. But Chopper was still charging about like a spring chicken. A headless spring chicken admittedly but – for him – incredibly lively. Luke had never seen him try so hard. Obviously he thought his place wasn't safe after the Wolves game. He needed to make an impression.

As the last seconds ticked away, Chopper's team gave away a corner. Up jogged Gaffer Mann and Cool Frederick, who were playing together in central defence – just as they probably would on Saturday. "Go on, son," Benny called to Luke. "You take it. In your boots. See how it feels."

Luke trotted across to the corner flag, noticing Frederick bend and touch his left shin. It was a signal they'd worked out in the park. Frederick would pretend to move for a ball dropped in short at the near post, but suddenly spin away. Luke then had to aim for the penalty spot, where Frederick would rise to nod it in. Strangely, Chopper wasn't hustling and barging him. In fact he stood about five steps behind. But he was eyeing Frederick's back in a dark way. The kind of way Luke's mum looked at the cat when it had just messed on her bed.

Luke began his run-up. The penalty box then fizzed into life before he put boot to ball. As soon as Frederick spun away, Gaffer Mann made a near-post run, and Chopper charged at him. He seemed to have his eyes shut tight. Luke lashed in the corner: as sweet a kick as he'd ever hit in trainers.

The ball cleared Gaffer's head. Frederick stopped short, jumped – and headed it firmly past Madman. But hardly anyone cheered the goal. All eyes were on the near post, where Chopper had continued his blind run and clattered poor Gaffer Mann. He'd wanted to make an impression, and now he surely had. Luke had heard of following through, but this tackle came out the other side.

At once Benny blew for time and came running on to check the damage. Gaffer had to be stretchered off, a bleeding gash all down his left thigh. Chopper was full of apologies but he seemed more surprised than sorry. And Luke – who had seen it all from out by the corner flag – had a horrible feeling he knew why.

Chopper had hit the wrong guy. He hadn't been planning to take *Gaffer* out. That trademark tackle had been meant for Frederick – the new threat to his place in the team. But if Luke's suspicions were right, Chopper's bit of GBH had still got him a result. Gaffer would never be fit enough to make the team on Saturday now. So Chopper would still play – *alongside* Cool Frederick. Creepy.

9

It was nine-fifteen at the Philistine and Firkin pub. Supporters Club Chairman Rocky Mitford smiled and held out the microphone. All evening he'd been making the punters pay up front to hear one Albion player after another make a monkey of himself on the Karaoke. Now they'd just filled the hat for Luke.

Luke gulped. He'd never really been a singer. He sometimes had a shout in the shower. He'd joined in with *'Ere we go, 'Ere we go, 'Ere we go!* on the South Side terrace at Ash Acre. But that was about it.

"Go on, Luke," said his dad, nudging him up from their table. "You're my kid, remember. Music's in your blood. You'll knock 'em dead!" That was the problem. With his dad's kind of music in his blood, he really might slaughter this poor unsuspecting audience.

"Do it, man," grinned Cool Frederick from behind his shades, even though the functions room was almost pitch black except for the small stage area. "You'll be ace."

"You can laugh," Luke said, as he headed for the spotlight. "It'll be your turn soon."

The three hundred or so supporters gave him a rousing welcome. Perhaps they thought the worst was past. Or maybe they were just too over-refreshed to care any more. But it hadn't been a joyride so far. Benny Webb crooning Frank Sinatra's "My Way" ("One-nils, I've had a few...") was bad enough. Chrissie Pick screaming "Firestarter" *his* way nearly cleared the room. Then there was the grisly sight of Chopper Foggon stomping about and grunting a tune that seemed to be called "Somebody's Gonna Get Their Head Kicked in Tonight".

"Is that a real song?" a gobsmacked Luke had asked. "Or is he just making it up as he goes along."

"No, it's real," Cool Frederick shot back at once. "Fleetwood Mac: 1969 B-side to 'Man of the World'. Got to number two." You could write everything Frederick didn't know about music on the spine of one CD box. In his spare time he ran a rare records search service from his home.

After a brief chat with Rocky, Luke agreed to do a Beatles number. "Yellow Submarine". That would give his dad a buzz, and since it was a Ringo song he wouldn't really have to sing. As it turned out, he only had to do a couple of lines, then the whole audience stormed in too. It sounded dire but no life was lost – and no one asked for their money back. Mission accomplished.

Back at his table, Luke breathed a huge sigh of relief. Soon he was ducking for cover, though. Madman was up.

Luke had never in his life heard anything like this. The song he chose was fair enough: "Jet" ("Paul McCartney and Wings," nodded Cool Frederick. "1974.") But once he'd struggled through the first verse, he branched off into a run-through of jet-engine sounds from Sir Frank Whittle's time to the present day. Listening to Madman's aircraft noises was tough when he didn't have a microphone. *With* one, it was unbearable.

No one protested when two of Chopper's mates jumped up from their table and dragged the Karaoke Keeper offstage before he could break the sound barrier. Luke had been watching that little party all evening – refuelling on lager like there was no tomorrow, slapping one another around just for the fun of it. Surprisingly, one of them was Mr Bates, his school's short-fused caretaker.

"Now isn't *that* an ugly-looking bunch of goons?" said a voice behind Luke. He pulled his head from under the table to find Agent Neil Veal standing there – all gold teeth and gel and a big Boss suit that he still seemed to be growing into.

Now the hat had gone round for Frederick. As soon as the Cool One vacated his seat between Luke and his dad, Agent Veal slipped into it as deftly as Harry Kewell feints away from a marker. "As I say," he went on, pulling a sheaf of papers and a pen out of his jacket pocket, "You wouldn't want to meet those boys in a dark alley." He tapped his nose. "They've all done bird, you know?"

"*Prison?*" said Luke. "Chopper Foggon? Batesy the Caretaker? What for?"

"Little bit of this. Little bit of that." He frowned. "Quite a lot of that, actually. Long time ago now. But as they say: you can take the man out of the prison but you can't take the prison out of the man." He grinned, and Luke wondered if Rodney knew about Mr Bates's record. His stepdad was a parent governor – surely the school hadn't knowingly hired an ex-con?

"Now – these papers. *If* I could just have your signature here, Mr Green, I can add Luke to my roster." Veal tried to hand Luke's dad the pen – hoping *he* had refuelled so completely that he would forget they hadn't actually struck a deal yet. It didn't work. Luke's dad folded his arms. "There are three other offers on the table," he said. "I've got to be sure my boy's gonna get the best representation."

Agent Veal smiled. He was about to launch into why he was by far the best bet for Luke's long-term career-and-merchandising development, when a sharp fizzy electronic din blitzed round the room. Rocky and Frederick were having real trouble with the mike, tossing it back and forth like a hot coal.

"Sorry about that, chaps," boomed big-voiced Rocky. "Our goalkeeper's 'song' seems to have had an adverse effect on the sound system. Still, here for your continued entertainment is Castle Albion's newest young star: central defender Frederick Dulac – with Kylie Minogue's 'I Should Be So Lucky'."

A storm of protest went up from just about every table. "*Refund! Refund!*" were the most polite cries that bounced around the smoke-filled room. Late eighties teen-pop was clearly not the hardcore Castle Albion supporters' cup of Bovril. But when Frederick's own backing track began, they soon shut up.

The beat was slowed right down. It sounded eerie, funky, chunky, *good*. Frederick stood stone-still in his shades and big kagoul with its fur-lined hood up, holding the mike in just two fingers in front of his face. And when he started his half-sung, half-spoken rap, Luke *heard* the hairs go up on the back of every single punter's neck.

51

It was like Liam Gallagher crossed with Massive Attack, and a bit of R Kelly thrown in on top. God knew what the actual words were, but the sheer sound was awesome. Even Luke's spellbound dad was plainly rethinking his view of post-sixties' pop. And already Luke could hear the cash tills clinking inside Agent Veal's head.

To say Frederick had the audience in the palm of his hand was ridiculous. He had them on the tip of his little finger. *"I should be so lucky... Lucky... Lucky... Lucky..."* he moaned every time the chorus came, bowing his head as if he was about to be executed. Unique, magnetic, electrifying. Cool.

When it was over the supporters went ape. You could forget about a refund. They were shelling out all over again – and this time the notes looked a whole lot browner than blue.

"Monster," Luke heard Neil Veal purring as he headed straight for the stage. "The boy's monster. He needs an agent."

As Frederick came down, the goggle-eyed Veal reached up to shake his hand – then he snatched the dodgy mike to make an announcement of his own. Frederick tried to warn him but too late.

Luke had never seen anyone electrocute himself before. Agent Veal's hair *did* briefly stand on end, like in the cartoons. And he *did* go blue around the edges as he juddered in mid-air before dropping the mike and coming back to earth.

But Neil Veal was a pro. He could take a volt or two. Still quivering, he picked up the mike – with two fingertips now – and flashed his metallic teeth out at the audience. "Ladies and gentlemen," he shakily announced. "I give you the mega-stunning Frederick Dulac! All enquiries, please, through me."

10

"Hey Boss," Carl Davey called across the dressing room. "Couldn't we get a new player with all that dosh Frederick made the other night."

"Yeah," Craig Edwards yelled back at him. "How about a decent striker?"

"Dwight Yorke might be up for it," suggested Dennis Meldrum. "Or Zola."

"What've they got that I haven't got?" Carl shouted.

"Where d'you want us to start?" Narris and Half-Fat chorused.

"Lads! Lads!" Benny Webb cut in. "That's enough of that." He nodded across at Carl. "Are you ready for it then?" The striker nodded back, teeth clenched, jaw set. "All right, Craig. Let him have it."

Everyone watched in awe as the pineapple rocketed out of the full-back's hand and belted into the waiting buttock. "Thank you," said Carl with a polite bow – after a scream that must have poleaxed the Scarborough boys next door.

"OK, OK, OK," said Benny. Team-talk time.

Luke sat up straighter on the bench, staring down at the gleaming Predators. His feet felt really weird again inside them. He'd already skidded over on the dressing-room floor, and luckily Frederick had caught him. He only hoped it would be easier out on the grass.

At least it hadn't been too hard getting to the game. He'd told his mum the school was running an extra Biology session for the year's high-flyers. She'd hummed and haahed but eventually let him go.

"Right then," said the Sheepskin Supremo, "Scarborough. What do we know about them?"

"That they're rubbish," laughed Madman, bouncing a ball between his feet.

"*What?*" rasped Benny, stepping closer to him.

Madman was concentrating on the ball so he didn't see the fury on Benny's face. "Well it stands to reason, Boss. They're second from bottom of the table."

"And where are we?" Benny was standing right over him now.

"*Third* from bottom!" Happily he went on bouncing. No one else said a word.

"So what does that make us? *A class act?*" As the ball came up from its last bounce, Benny swung out a foot and hoofed it away into a startled Chrissie Pick's hands.

"Madman would've dropped that," Narris said under his breath.

"Sorry, Boss," Madman answered, suddenly realizing he'd put his foot in it.

"Sorry, Boss *indeed*! You must *never* underestimate the opposition. You must *always* give 'em respect! Is that clear to all of you?" He crossed the floor again.

"Yes, Boss." "Right, Boss." "You said it, Boss." "We hear you, Boss."

"But they didn't beat Villa and Wolves, did they, Boss?" Madman said, just low enough for Benny not to hear. Chopper stamped on his foot anyway.

Benny went on to give every player a highly-detailed briefing, finishing up with Frederick. "I want to see a telepathic understanding between you and Chopper, son," he said at the end. "Keep talking to each other, right?"

Luke saw a puzzled look flit across Frederick's face. He knew why. Telepathy meant reading each other's minds, not speaking. But Frederick was way too cool to point that out. "OK then," said Benny as everyone got up. "One more thing you might like to chew on. This lot – Scarborough – they only came into the League in 1987. And d'you know why? They was the first club to get automatic promotion by winning the

Conference. Some other team's gonna win it this year – and they're gonna take the place of the bottom team in *our* League. And if we don't get some flippin' points soon, that'll be *us*! Now get out there and don't take no prisoners!"

It was a bumper crowd for a League fixture. Well over 5,000 – mainly because there were vouchers in the matchday programme for tickets for the upcoming Newcastle game. Some of the Albion fans were already wearing Ruud Gullit-style dreadlocks painted blue and white.

There wasn't much for them to shout about in the first forty-five, though. In fact the handful of red-and-black travellers at the away end were soon making more noise.

"You Really Aren't A
Very Good Team At All!"

they kept chanting at the Albion (or words to that effect). They weren't far wrong.

As almost any ITV commentator would have put it, it was a case of "After the Lord Mayor's Show". They'd turned over Wolves on the big stage. Now in this bread-and-butter fixture they couldn't string two passes together. Sad to say, Luke was struggling too. After five minutes he started getting blisters. After fifteen he could hardly run and, every time he tried to lay the ball off, his studs stuck in the soggy turf. But according to a furious Benny Webb at half-time, he was still Albion's second-best player – after Cool Frederick.

"At least Luke's trying," the manager roared. "And this new kid reads the game so well, he's probably left a bookmark out on the pitch! But you other nine – you're *illegible*!" He meant illiterate but Frederick, fiddling with a plastic bag in his kagoul pocket, let it pass. Benny ranted plenty more. It didn't make a great deal of difference after the break.

"You're Technically Incompetent And You're Fully Aware Of It!"

yelled the delighted away fans (or words to that effect), as Ruel and Dennis and Craig and Narris and Carl kept on struggling to find their touch. Chrissie and Half-Fat weren't getting any touches at all.

And then there was Chopper.

Luke didn't know what to make of *his* performance. He made his usual number of unforced errors and mistimed tackles. But from the word go he'd been amazingly, almost supernaturally, quiet. Perhaps he really was trying to communicate telepathically with Frederick. He certainly kept looking at him. But if his expression was anything to go by, all his messages ran along the lines of "I'll have you, you small illegitimate person!" (or words to that effect).

Which was odd because they were meant to

be on the same side. And psychotic though Chopper was, he usually remembered to direct his malice, bile and venom only at members of the opposing team. But then in the seventy-third minute something happened which made Luke wonder whose side Chopper *was* on.

The phrase "hospital pass" was well-known at Luke's school. The gym teacher was always using it when they played touch-rugby. It meant giving a team-mate such a bad pass, he was bound to crash into an opponent in trying to reach it – and would probably wind up in hospital. And now Chopper Foggon unveiled the Mother Of All Hospital Passes.

It began harmlessly enough. The Scarborough keeper sent a long punt upfield. Their lone striker went for it, trapped it, and tried to twist round. But Frederick was jockeying him so expertly that he just couldn't turn, and in the end he ran the ball into touch over by the corner flag. So far, so good.

Craig fetched the ball for the throw. Chopper wanted it on the edge of the penalty area. And what Chopper wanted, he usually got. Miraculously he controlled it first time. But instead of looking ahead for Ruel or Carl, he glanced at Frederick, who was moving quickly upfield while one of the Scarborough midfielders came forward to close him down.

Luke saw the look on the hard man's face. He read it as plain as day. *Pick the bones out of this one, cool boy*, it said. And with an awesome accuracy that Luke had never seen from Chopper before, he stroked the ball to a point exactly halfway between the advancing Frederick and the oncoming midfielder. Hospital pass? This one came with a bunch of grapes, a bouquet of flowers and a Get Well Soon card chucked in for good measure.

There was no way Frederick could get to it without lunging full-length. Ditto, the Scarborough man. Both flew through the air, determined not to lose out, and made bone-jarring contact with the ball at exactly the same time. You could hear the crowd and all twenty other players gasp at the impact. It could have been catastrophic if Frederick hadn't used his brain so fast.

Instead of letting his momentum carry him on into his opposite number, he somehow fell to the side, while shooting out his *other* foot to nick the ball away and back to Chopper. But Chopper wasn't expecting a return pass. He was just standing there watching, hands on his hips, idly wondering what time the hospital would be open for visitors. As the ball rolled slowly towards him, he didn't seem to see it. But the lone Scarborough striker did.

Lurking on the edge of the penalty box, he should have been offside. But Chopper was keeping him *on*side by staying rooted to the spot. In he nipped. Intercepting Frederick's pass, he nudged it past the statue-like Chopper, ran round the other side of him, drew Madman out and poked it through his legs into the net. The Boro were ahead. A gift goal? Short of wrapping it up in silver paper and tying a bow around it, Chopper could not have been more generous.

Albion had just over a quarter of an hour left to put the damage right. But they never really looked like pulling it off. Luke and Frederick were both limping a bit – Luke with his blisters, Frederick from the tackle. They put in one hundred and ten per cent effort to carve out an equalizer. But goals scored from inside your own half are pretty rare in football – and Scarborough, sniffing victory, made sure they kept most of the play in Albion's part of the pitch.

Benny went into hand-signal overdrive on the line. The crowd did its best to lift the home side. But it wasn't to be. When the whistle went, Scarborough had notched up their first away win of the season – and in the process swapped League positions with the team they'd just whipped. Only one club – Shrewsbury – now stood between Castle Albion and the Nation-wide League's trapdoor.

"*That was an absolutely wretched perfor-mance!*" (Or words to that effect) Benny Webb stormed in the dressing room. He even changed the habit of a managing lifetime and hurled a teacup from half-time at the wall. It never got that far, though. Albion could only afford Styro-foam cups so it dropped short – into Chopper Foggon's lap, spilling dregs.

The room went silent. You didn't chuck tea at Chopper even if he *had* just shot his own team in the foot. But he didn't appear to notice. All his attention was on Frederick who was sitting directly opposite and twisting around to fiddle again with that small plastic bag in his kagoul pocket. For some reason Chopper's face sud-denly lit up. Then he stood and rocketed out of the room.

"That's the fastest he's moved all afternoon," muttered Chrissie Pick.

"You should've done that at half-time, Boss," said Carl. "When it was still hot."

"Never mind," Madman chipped in. "Gaffer'll be back next week."

"Yeah," Half-Fat hissed in Luke's ear. "But will Benny *dare* to axe Chopper?"

Luke didn't have time to hang around and discuss future team-selection. His mum had wanted him back for tea at five, so he had precisely six minutes to get home. Pulling on his school clothes over his kit, he checked with Benny that training was at Ash Acre on Wednesday, then made his getaway.

But something held him up as he unlocked his bike in the car park. Over in a corner, hidden from the dejected fans who were dragging themselves out of the ground, Luke saw Chopper Foggon from behind: broad shoulders hunched, bullet head bowed. For an awful moment Luke thought he was taking revenge for the tea-dregs incident by having a wee on Benny Webb's old Volvo. But on tiptoeing closer, he saw that Chopper was in conversation.

As he talked – fifteen to the dozen – the other guy made rapid notes on a pad. Luke knew his face. His picture was often in the *Evening Argus*. He wasn't Clyde Bastopol, the regular football correspondent. This was Rupert "Sniffer" Turdock: muck-raking journalist extraordinary. If there was ever a whiff of sleaze within a radius of fifty miles, Sniffer's nostrils caught it first. But what on earth could Albion's hard man be wafting his way? Luke tiptoed closer still.

Chopper sensed someone behind him. (Why couldn't he ever sense opposition strikers like that?) Swinging around, he caught sight of Luke and went rabid. Jabbing a big stubby finger his way, he bellowed: "Oi! You! *No!* Clear off back to your playpen!'' Then he turned and stepped towards Luke, smiling with menace. ''And if I get any grief out of you,'' he said more softly, before erupting: *''Then I'll tell your mum where you've been all afternoon! RIGHT?''*

''Right,'' Luke agreed quickly, backing off. But he didn't have long to wait to find out what kind of beans the man in the tea-stained shorts had been spilling to Sniffer Turdock.

12

As Luke was leaving school on Tuesday he bumped into Cool Frederick. They hadn't seen each other since the game. Luke's mate was just on his way *in*.

Cool F's timetable wasn't like anyone else's at school. It wasn't like anyone's *anywhere*. As long as he kept getting his work in on time – and getting straight A's for pretty well all of it – the staff let him come and go as he chose. That gave him lots of time to run his rare records search service. In fact he was taking a mobile call from another satisfied customer as he stopped to high-five Luke.

"Yo," he grinned, nodding at Luke's blistered feet. "Still limping?"

"You're not exactly dancing around, yourself," Luke shot back. Someone as cool as Frederick could never actually hobble but the after-effects of that tackle were still quite clear. "That pass from Chopper was diabolical," Luke went on. "I'm sure he meant it too. He *wanted* you to get crocked."

Frederick just raised an eyebrow. Why bother with words when your eyebrow could do it all? This particular angle said: I appreciate your concern, Luke, but I really don't think you need to worry. Chopper's such an inaccurate passer of the ball, he could never have hit that spot on purpose. Forget it.

"But then there was that chop on Gaffer Mann in training," Luke argued back. "I saw it all. Chopper was going for *you*. He had it all lined up. It was just that you moved so fast, he hacked down the wrong bloke."

Frederick widened his eyes. *This* look said: Again, thanks for the concern. But even if what you're saying is right, I think I can look after myself.

Before Luke could say any more, a gaggle of glory-supporter girls giggled past. All carrying Liverpool and Chelsea and Man U bags, they whistled and pointed at Luke and Frederick. After they'd gone by they sang over their shoulders:

"*Down* To The Conference!
You're Goin' *Down* To The Conference!"

Luke had taken plenty of stick from his teachers that day too. "Everyone who played in a humbling home defeat by lowly Scarborough stand up *now*!" barked the IT student before they switched on their computers. And the art

67

teacher had drawn a big sketch of a goal-shaped grave and put *Castle Albion RIP* on it.

"I'm serious," Luke told Frederick, getting back to the point. "You've got to look out for Chopper. He thinks you're a threat and he's a right headcase." He lowered his voice. "You know he's done time inside, don't you?"

Just as Luke said that, another ex-con came out from behind the bike sheds and stalked their way: Mr Bates the caretaker, Chopper's mate from the Karaoke night – lanky, shaven-headed, a rolled-up local newspaper in his hand.

As usual he looked well wound-up. Never in the field of school caretaking had one man gone so mental so many times about so little. Like Chopper, Mr Bates could start a fight in an empty room. But at least Chopper then won them – Mr Bates was lucky to scrape a draw. He really wasn't the brightest guy on earth: several bristles short of the full broom. But a bit of bad news always made his day.

"Oi – you!" he yelled at Frederick, waving the *Argus* like a truncheon. "You're for it now! You're gonna get a real slap!"

Frederick gave him a lazy smile, then his mobile rang again and he turned away to take the call. Luke watched the caretaker lope closer, still waving the newspaper. He was probably going to have a go about Albion's wretched display on Saturday. Somebody must have read out the match report to him – he surely couldn't read himself. "Hello, Mr Bates," Luke said. "What's up?"

"The *game*'s up," he sneered, unrolling the paper. "*His* little game's up!" He jabbed a finger at Frederick's back. "What do you say about *this* then, nipper?"

Surprisingly, he didn't hold up the back page for Luke to see. The paragraph in question was bang on the front, under a bigger piece head-lined *Mercy-Dash Cat In Lottery Jinx Drama*. Luke's jaw dropped as his eyes flew over the few lines:

YOUNG ALBION STAR IN STIMULANTS QUIZ
According to an unnamed source close to Castle Albion FC, one of the club's new young stars, Frederick Dulac, uses artificial stimulants – even for training (allegedly). No Albion player in the club's history has ever failed a drugs test. "It's the only kind of test some of our boys would pass," quipped Albion physio Terry Vaudeville. Manager Benny Webb was unavailable for comment but doubtless he will go head-to-head with Dulac on this well before the Newcastle Cup-tie.

Aghast, Luke looked from the paper to Frederick's back as Mr Bates made windy harumphing noises. "State of youth today," he grunted. "No damn respect. What they need's a spell in the army..." The usual stuff.

Frederick was blissfully unaware of any trouble. "No sweat," he was telling his caller. (Even *he* couldn't do eyes and eyebrows on the phone). "Sure, I can track down old Eurovision Song Contest winners for you – which ones? *All* of them...?"

Mr Bates smiled a nasty smile at him. "You've shot your bolt now, sunshine," he snorted, then turned and marched away in search of more bad news.

Frederick finished his call. "Gotta go," he said to Luke, tapping his bag. "Get this Geography map work in." Already he was moving off.

"No, wait!" Luke cried, starting after him. "Oh blimey, look. I ... I think you're being stitched up..."

"*LUKE!*" An unearthly roar from the school gates stopped both boys in their tracks. Then Luke swivelled round to find his mum half-in, half-out of the Escort. She ferried him back and forth to school every day – just to make sure he didn't have *any* contact with footballers, managers or agents. Now she stabbed her finger at her watch to show she had been waiting for – oh – at least fifteen seconds. If it got to twenty, Luke was dead meat.

"I'll ring you tonight," he called out to Frederick before rushing up to the car. "OK?"

13

Luke tried Frederick fourteen times that evening. Home *and* mobile. Every time, he drew a blank. In the end he got fed up leaving messages. Then his own phone went. Rodney snatched it up. "Ah," he said slowly, "Mr Mallard..."

Luke went rigid on the sofa. There *was* no Mr Mallard. This was a code-name Rodney had invented three weeks before – for use in emergencies only. Mallard – Duck – Webbed Feet – *Webb*. That was the way Rodney's mind worked. And now he was sitting right next to Luke's mum talking to Benny!

"No, Mr Mallard. I'm afraid I can't help you there. No. Oh I see. Well, yes, Saturday would be far better. Yes, Saturday will be fine. Till Saturday, then."

Luckily Luke's mum was distracted. The costume-drama video they were watching had cut to Blenheim Palace and she was craning her neck to get a closer look at the landscaped gardens. "Who was that?" she snapped softly.

"Oh, just Mallard from the office, dear. Trouble with some *paper*work." He widened his eyes at Luke on the first two syllables of that last word. "I'll sort it out before the meeting on Saturday."

Luke guessed it was about Albion's next away game. But he had to wait almost an hour before his mum went to the loo and he could talk privately with Rodney. "So what did Benny want?" he hissed.

"Who, not what. Frederick. He wanted to know where he was. Didn't sound too pleased. And he asked if I'd seen the *Argus* tonight. What's happening, Luke?"

Luke wasn't keen to discuss this with his stepdad. Not yet anyway. He'd already worried Rodney stiff by telling him Mr Bates had done bird – allegedly. And the older generation always went a bit funny when it came to drugs, even if this whole thing was a put-up job. But now he saw no way out. Quickly he filled in Rodney on the *Argus* article. "It's down to the Chopper," he whispered. "It has to be. I saw him with Sniffer Turdock after the last game. He'll do anything to get Frederick out of the team. Even shop him to the press."

"Well, I sincerely hope that's the explanation," Rodney whispered back, his face very long, his eyes very big behind his glasses. Yes, he'd gone a bit funny.

"What was that stuff about Saturday?" Luke went on. He heard his mum coming out of the upstairs loo.

Rodney paused before answering. His mind was still on the drugs. Fatally, it made him drop his guard. "Oh, he was just checking that I'll be able to get you to the match..."

"*Match?*" She'd heard. From halfway down the stairs she'd picked it up. And she didn't think Rodney was whispering about the things you light fires with. Coming into the room, she squinted at the two of them as if they'd been plotting to turn the house into an enormous Subbuteo pitch.

"Yes, dear," Rodney rushed to cover up his horrible blunder. "Mr *Graham* Match. I was just telling Luke about him – you know? – the client I'm meeting on Saturday. He lives in Rotherham, you remember? Not very far at all from your parents' place in Doncaster. So – as we agreed earlier – I'll drop Luke with them around lunchtime, then go straight on to my meeting. It'll be so nice for him to be able to spend time alone with his grandparents, won't it?"

"I didn't know your client's name was ... *Match*," she said as she prowled past them, resumed her seat, then pressed the Play button again. She smelled a rat, there was no doubt about it. She sensed that something was up – and when she had even the faintest

73

suspicion, she usually took swift preventative action.

Luke watched the rest of the boring video with both sets of fingers crossed behind his back. Oh Rodney, *Rodney*! It really might go either way now. With just one word, his mum could wreck their Saturday gameplan. It was supposed to have gone like this: Albion were away at mid-table Rotherham. By a fluke Rodney's firm *did* have a client in that town. And by an even bigger fluke, Luke's nan and grandpa lived in nearby Doncaster – and they were mad keen to see Luke play. So three hours before, Rodney had sorted it. He'd told Luke's mum he had a vital meeting in Yorkshire. Then he'd rung the old folks to say their grandson would be "paying them a visit". Luke's mum had swallowed the whole story. Everything had looked hunky-dory. Then Rodney had gone and dropped his clanger. As Ruud Gullit would say: very sloppy.

Yet by Luke's bedtime, his mum still hadn't said anything. Once he was in bed he uncrossed his fingers. (Maybe, on reflection, he should have done that *before* trying to clean his teeth.) It looked like it was going to be OK after all.

On *her* way to bed, his mum paused outside his door. "Goodnight, Luke," she said, unusually warmly. "I've just rung your nan and grandpa. They understood perfectly when I told them I didn't fancy spending the weekend here on my own. Rodney can call in to see them but you'll stay with me. We'll have some quality time together. They're selling off gnomes cheap down at the garden centre this Saturday: you can help me get them home. You'll love it."

Then she was gone. And with her, so were all Luke's hopes for Saturday. And poor old Rodney still had to drive right up to Doncaster and back. Sloppy or what?

14

During the taxi ride to Ash Acre the next morning, Luke's head was a mess. How was he going to break it to Benny that he couldn't play at Rotherham? Where had Cool Frederick been last night? Was Chopper Foggon really behind the substance-scandal? Suddenly there seemed to be a lot more problems in the world than the fact that Castle Albion were twenty-third in the Division Three table.

Some reporters were skulking outside the players' entrance. They burst into life when they saw the midfield playmaker and closed on him like stewards around a streaker. "Tell us, Luke, has your mate been suspended by the club?" "Luke, what's the word on Madman – is *he* on something too?" "Our readers are desperate to know, Luke: Will you ever play studless again?"

"No comment, no comment, no comment," Luke murmured. God, the media.

The atmosphere inside the ground seemed

very solemn. In the club offices no one was talking. The secretaries waved to Luke but didn't smile. Then as he turned into the second corridor on the way to the dressing room, he almost tripped over Carl Davey. The striker – already changed – was squatting by the door, peering bamboozled into his kitbag and shaking his head.

"What's wrong, Carl?" Luke asked as he passed. "Forgot your chewing gum?"

For a moment Carl appeared not to hear. He went on shaking his head but he was staring at the wall now. Maybe it was serious – and something really awful had happened. Luke kicked himself for that crack about the chewing gum.

"Tell me, Carl. Is it ... is it to do with this Frederick stuff?"

Still squatting, Carl turned a woeful face on his team-mate. "I can't understand it," he said in a voice to match. "I cannot understand it. It doesn't make any sense..."

"*What*, Carl?" Luke put a consoling hand on his shoulder.

In reply, the striker dipped a hand into his bag, pulled out a squishy-looking pineapple, and held it up like Exhibit A at a murder trial.

"How could it *happen*?" he asked Luke, wide-eyed. "Every other time I've taken a hit before a game I've scored. Nothing was different on

Saturday. We did everything just the same. So how come I didn't get a goal?" He groaned. "It's beyond belief!"

"You can say that again," sighed Luke, heading on to the dressing room.

But it was like a funeral in there too. Everyone was sitting along three of the walls staring stonily at the floor. Only Madman was looking up – at the physio's bench where by rights he should have been cranking up his latest aircraft impression. He winked at Luke but it was a jaded wink.

Then Luke saw Benny. He was standing behind the door, arms folded, face like thunder. He looked just like Luke's mum when she was waiting to roar at the milkman that one of yesterday's pints was off. (Only she didn't have the sheepskin coat. Or the beard.) "Where is he?" growled Benny as Luke went to his peg.

Luke froze. "Who, Boss?"

"Your mate! I've been tryin' to get hold of him all night and all morning. Don't he ever go home? What is it with him – parties? All-night raves?"

"No, Boss," came a new voice from the doorway. "I had to shoot across to Amsterdam. See a man about a record." Everyone's eyes turned to Frederick.

"A *criminal* record, eh?" jeered Chopper Foggon. But no one laughed. "Go on, Boss.

Carpet him. Chuck the book at him. Tell him he's all washed up."

Frederick frowned at Benny, puzzled. Here it came: the head-to-head. Sheepskin v Kagoul. Hot-Under-The-Collar versus Very-Cool-Indeed. Frederick obviously didn't have a clue what this was about. Benny saw that too and began to shake his head. "Haven't you seen what was in the paper, son?"

Frederick frowned harder. He still had his kagoul hood up. When he glanced at Luke, his mate flashed him an *I-did-try-to-tell-you* look.

"It's ugly," Benny told him. "An ugly allegation. Someone's fingered you for substance abuse, son. Artificial stimulants. Even before training, they say." He closed his eyes as if the entire Nationwide League had just come to rest on his shoulders. "I can't tell you how devastated I'd be if it's true. I run a clean ship at this club. Always have, always will. Drugs is for mugs – that's my motto and no one's gonna change it. So I'll ask you once, son, and I want a dead straight, no-mess answer: are you – or have you ever been – on anything?"

There was a moment's pause. No one in the dressing room breathed. No one could look full-on at Frederick either. No one but Benny and Luke. And Luke saw a smile spread across the Cool Boy's face that answered in neon letters:

You've gotta be crazy to think that! He didn't have to say a word. Just smile.

Across he went to his peg, slid out of his kagoul and hung it up. A rumble of relief went round the room. No one looked more bucked up than Benny himself. But it wasn't over yet. Chopper Foggon raised a nicotine-stained finger and pointed it at Frederick's kagoul. "What's that in his pocket?"

Benny went over. Frederick stood aside. The manager reached in and took out a small transparent sandwich bag. The sort Luke took his packed lunch to school in. But this one didn't have underboiled-egg sandwiches and a satsuma inside. It was half-full of white powder.

"*That's* what he went to Amsterdam for!" Chopper spat. "I've seen him fiddling about with bags like that in here before."

Benny turned to Frederick. He could hardly speak. "Son, is this drugs?"

Instead of answering, Frederick took the bag, snapped it open, put a finger in then licked the dollop of white stuff off the end of it. "Kickin'," he grinned at Benny, looking him straight in the eye. "Be my guest."

As if mesmerized, Benny put a finger in too. First he looked at what he pulled out. Then he sniffed it. Then, very gingerly, he dabbed a bit on his tongue. His face split apart in a smile wide enough to drive a team bus down. "*Sherbet!*"

80

"Way to go," Frederick explained as everyone (except Chopper) fell about laughing. "I'm not cool with the liquorice on the dips so I empty the tubes out." He took the bag from Benny and stuck in another finger. "Easier access too."

"OK, OK, OK!" yelled Benny above the delighted uproar. "Problem solved. Good on ya, Frederick son. I *thought* you wasn't a wrong 'un. Now let's get back to the business in hand: winning three points at Rotherham on Saturday. We're all up for *that* one now, aren't we?"

This had to be the moment – while Benny was still so chuffed. Luke raised his hand. "Sorry, Boss," he winced. "I won't be able to make it."

For the next five minutes everyone (except Chopper) tried to suggest ways to get Luke to Millmoor and back without his mum finding out. They drew a blank. It just wasn't going to happen. Not this weekend. And Benny had to live with it.

"We'll miss you, son," he said. "We'll miss you big-time. But the week after: the Newcastle Cup-tie down here – you're on for *that*, right?"

"He'll be here," Cool Frederick winked. "We'll sort it between us. Bit more Extra Biology. Special half-term weekend session, yeah?" Then before he put his bag away, he offered a lick of sherbet to anyone who wanted it, including Chopper – who was *not* a very happy bunny. He didn't look as if he'd got out of bed the wrong side. More as if he'd taken a circular saw to the mattress and hit the floor that way.

Luke didn't like that look. The Chopper wasn't finished yet. He'd be back.

Saturdays weren't meant for this. Luke looked around in bewilderment. It was as if he had slipped into some bizarre parallel world. A world where no one cared how Brighton were doing at home to Swansea, or if Rochdale had pulled one back at Darlington. Not one of these people had a naff little pennant in their car with a beloved club's name emblazoned on it. None of them owned a treasured autograph of ex-Swindon boss Jolly John Gorman. To each of these people, life was entirely liveable without football. All that mattered to them, all they really wanted from a Saturday afternoon was ... garden gnomes.

"What do you think of this one, Luke?" his mum asked quietly, almost reverently, leading him through the garden centre to yet another little pot-bellied statuette, this one holding a fishing rod. Luke was tempted to say it looked like Gazza, only a little bit slimmer.

"Very nice," he replied, glancing at his watch.

Four twenty-seven. Up at Rotherham the game had entered its last quarter. Luke's need to know the score was chewing his insides to pieces, spitting them out then chewing them up all over again. At four o'clock, thinking his mum wasn't looking, he'd slipped Rodney's headset over his ears and tuned in to the local radio station. Half-time. Still nil-nil! And Frederick was playing an absolute blinder. Then his mum had noticed, plucked the Walkman off his head and snapped it away in her handbag. She wanted her son's complete and utter attention.

"What do you think of his *expression*?" she asked about the fisherman.

"Very nice." Luke had said these same two words roughly fifty-six times. How on earth were you supposed to judge a garden gnome? What were the particular qualities to look for? His mum already had seventeen of them at home. Why did she need another five?

"Go and fetch one of those big trolleys," she said after a long pause to weigh up all the pros and cons. "I think I've made up my mind."

Luke trudged over to where the trolleys were racked together. Great heavy things. Struggling to pull the first one out, he heard an odd strangled sound, as if someone close by had just swallowed part of a shrub. Then he heard it again. He looked up. All he could see was a high wall of stacked-up yellow gro-bags.

"Luke," the wall of bags itself seemed to hiss. "It's me. *Here.*"

Baffled, Luke took a step closer. Behind, he could hear a radio playing. A commentary. A *football* commentary. Rotherham v Albion!

"Here," said the radio-owner's voice again. And Luke spotted a crack of daylight in the wall. In the same moment he recognized the voice. This was incredible. On a Saturday afternoon in a garden centre. Did the man never give up? Agent Neil Veal!

"Luke," he whispered quickly from his hidey-hole. "Good to touch base. I can see your mum's busy at this moment in time and I respect that. But she looks – well – just a *tad* happier than when I last tried to discuss terms with her. D'you think she might possibly see her way to giving me a moment? *After* she's finished gnoming, of course? I've got the papers with me. All I need is—"

"Not in a million years," Luke whispered back. "She'll never sign *anything* to do with football, can't you see? But hey, what's the score at Millmoor?"

"Still nil-nil. Chopper's having another complete mare. Frederick keeps bailing him out. Look Luke, if your mum *does* fancy a word I'll be here for a good while yet. Perhaps we could do Coke at the vending machine...?"

Shaking his head, Luke lugged the trolley

85

over to his mum. She gave him a really funny look. He guessed she'd seen him talking to the wall. (Well, Luke thought, people talk to plants, so why not to the gro-bags you put them in?) But she was too fired up about the gnomes to ask him why.

It took her another ten minutes, but finally she got the five she wanted on to the trolley. To Luke they looked a bit like Arsenal's back four plus David Seaman. On the way to the checkout they passed the big yellow wall. Luke's mum was out in front so as Luke went past the opening, he breathed: "Score?"

"We're one-nil down. Chopper own goal. No one near him. Sliced a cross into his own net. Now *is* your mum on for a free and frank exchange of views...?"

With his stomach lurching, Luke moved on. It must be injury time now. Another defeat was in the offing. The Conference was coming one step closer.

His mum paid for the gnomes, then walked next to Luke like a police escort as he pushed the trolley through the rain to the car. Glancing behind, Luke saw Agent Veal creeping towards the vending machine next to a row of discarded trolleys. Did he *really* think the woman was about to have a fizzy drink and a free-and-frank with him?

Luke loaded the gnomes into the boot of the

Escort. (Not only had Rodney had to drive all the way to Yorkshire; he'd also had to hire another car.) "Right," he said. "I'll take the trolley back." At least, that way, he could check out the final score with Neil Veal, who was now lurking behind the vending machine.

"No, that's OK," smiled his mum. She didn't lighten up often, but when she did, it was *always* at the wrong moments. "Let me do it." Still smiling, she started waltzing back through the puddles. At once Luke set off after her. He could see what would happen. Agent Veal would think she was coming across to talk. Sure enough, out popped his Raybanned head from behind the machine.

Frantically Luke waved at him to hide again. "No, *no!*" he mouthed. But Veal was too busy adjusting his mega-gelled hair and Boss suit lapels. Any second, Luke's mum would catch sight of him, recognize him, and then...

It never happened. Her pleasant moods didn't last for long. The rain was pouring harder. Why should she get even wetter by taking the trolley all the way back? With a mighty heave, she launched the thing forward, turned on her heel and waved at Luke to follow her. "Come on," she ordered him. "Let's go!"

Luke stood goggle-eyed. The moment Veal finished his grooming and looked up, the run-away trolley smashed into his midriff. He flew backwards into a display of bird-tables and mini tree-houses which immediately avalanched down on top of him.

Then from underneath, Luke heard a moan: "No probs... Just surface scratches..." A head poked out. "Oh, the game ended up one-nil. And hey, look – this is just a thought. Why not ask your mum if she'd prefer to let someone *else* do the negotiating for her? A third party? Anyone she likes. I'd be cool with that. *Yeah?* Brill!"

It was a ludicrous suggestion. But Veal's head was swaying so much, he seemed to think that Luke was nodding in agreement. Then the dizziness kicked in again and he sank back down into the wreckage, smiling.

16

Luke had never been in Frederick's house before. Theirs was more of a meet-on-the-street kind of friendship than a roam-round-the-home. He didn't manage to get inside on Sunday evening, either. "Are you sure this is the right place?" asked his dad, after Luke had rung the bell three times.

Luke nodded. He hadn't told Frederick he was going to drop by on his night with his dad. He hadn't been able to. Still no one was answering the home or mobile numbers. And he *had* to give his mate a wake-up call. That look on Chopper Foggon's face! Frederick didn't seem to realize the Chopper'd stop at nothing to keep his spot in the team. And after another mare at Rotherham – and with Gaffer fit again – he would almost certainly be axed against Newcastle. Unless, of course, he could somehow make sure Frederick was out of action.

They were just on their way back to Luke's

dad's van when the side gate opened. "Hey!" Frederick grinned coolly. "Whassup?"

"Frederick!" said Luke. "We were just passing and wondered if you were in."

Frederick turned up both palms as if to say: well, yes I am. Then he turned and tilted his head a tiny fraction, inviting them to follow.

They didn't go left into the house, but carried on down the garden to a different building altogether. Small but neat-looking, it was like a whole house in miniature. And when they got inside, that was what it turned out to be: lushly-carpeted lounge with a widescreen TV, kitchen, shower room, single upstairs bedroom – and another room at the back with its door open. Luke's music-mad dad edged over to it, lured by the rows of records, tapes and CDs that stretched from wall to wall. Then, like a man who was looking an angel in the face, he drifted inside.

"This is where I hang," Frederick said, shutting the outer door. "Now what can I get you, Mr Green? Peroni? Beck's? Budweiser?"

Before Luke's dad could answer, the phone on the bookcase rang. Frederick took no notice. "And you, Luke? What'll it be?"

"Well, how about answering the phone for starters?" Luke grinned.

Frederick's eyebrow moved. Luke wasn't one hundred per cent sure what this angle meant.

Maybe something like: answer it yourself, and see why I don't bother. Luke decided to do that anyway, while Frederick slunk through to the kitchen.

As soon as he picked up the receiver, a rumbling noise began at the other end. It took Luke a moment or two to gather that it was a voice, heavily-disguised – then a few moments more to make out any of the words. "We'll 'ave you, nipper," seemed to be the basic gist of it. "We're gonna *'ave* you..."

Luke's hand shook as he put down the phone. Somehow the voice was familiar. Not Chopper's, but familiar. "How long's that been going on?" he asked.

Frederick just shrugged. He handed Luke a Coke and took a lager through to the back room. Luke went in pursuit. "Have you told the police?"

"The *police*?" laughed the Cool One. "No way." The room was done out like a shop. Rack on rack of vinyl records in the centre; shelves of cassettes and CDs around the sides. Luke's dad was holding an old forty-five with a dark pink label. He looked as if he was about to go down on his knees and kiss it.

"The original 'Autumn Almanac' by The Kinks," he purred, turning it over. "And 'Mr Pleasant' on the flip. First record I ever bought! Lost it years ago now, of course. But this was the one. This was where, for me, the journey began."

"October 1967," Frederick nodded. "In the States 'Mr Pleasant' was actually an A-side. Got to number eighty. Look, I've got two more copies. Keep that one." He winked. "Early Valentine's Day present for tomorrow, right?"

Luke's dad did kiss the record's label then. And he toasted Frederick with his lager. "*I should be so lucky!*" he beamed from ear to ear.

"But what about the phone calls?" Luke persisted. "Chopper must be behind them. You've *got* to watch your back. You know how it is with him – it's not the winning, it's the taking apart."

"Whoa!" said Luke's dad, leafing through a pile of singles on a shelf. "What have we here? 'Making Your Mind Up', 'Waterloo', 'Save Your Kisses For Me'..."

"Eurovision Song Contest winners. New client. Guy in that big pad up on the Heights. James Prince, right – the kid who made the pile in computers? He wants me to nose out all the winners. I'm taking that first lot up tomorrow night. Why not come too, Luke? Meet the Majestic Man?"

Luke frowned. He'd heard of James Prince. Who hadn't? The founder of Majestic Software: Britain's Bill Gates, only younger – and apparently a whole lot nerdier. He'd made his first million from a new computer application when he was ten. God knew how much more he'd racked up since then. And what did he do with his cash? Pay Cool F to find him a job-lot of old Euro-trash.

"Do it, yeah?" Frederick laughed. "See how the other half lives?"

Luke chewed his lip. It might be worth going. If only so that Frederick wasn't on his own. This *could* just be another stitch-up. He would have to rope in Rodney too, though. His mum still didn't trust him to go anywhere solo. "All right," he said, "I'll see what I can do."

They stayed for another half-hour but whatever Luke said, he couldn't get Frederick to take Chopper seriously. He just wanted to play them some brand new Vietnamese hip-hop. Luke's dad politely pretended he liked it, but *his* head was still stuck in the Sixties like a toe up a bath-tap. And he was still rummaging through psychedelic album sleeves by Vanilla Fudge, Moby Grape and Heavy Sausage when Luke high-fived the Cool One and headed back to the street.

Standing at the gate waiting for his dad, Luke noticed a grubby white van dim its headlights. Its engine was running but it wasn't going anywhere. It hadn't been going anywhere for quite some time: Luke had seen it there, humming away, when he'd first turned up. Quickly he went back to the little house to drag his dad out. "Come and see. Come and see. There's this dodgy-looking van..."

But when they got outside the street was empty except for Luke's dad's gruesomely multi-coloured vehicle. "Must've been a mirage," his dad laughed. "A hallucination. A bad trip." But Luke knew it wasn't. He could smell the exhaust fumes. And they stank of Castle Albion's talent-free central defender.

17

Rodney wasn't mad keen on another drive. The weekend trip had taken a lot out of him. He'd managed to catch the Rotherham-Albion game but that had almost finished him off. (Chopper's own-goal was even more shocking than one of John Barnes's jackets, he'd said.) Now he had to drive Luke and Frederick up to the Heights. "What'll we tell your mum?" he whined in the kitchen.

"Say we're going to look at some owls. Oh, go on, Rodney. Then we *could* look for some owls afterwards." Luke decided to lie through his teeth. "Frederick reckons he heard one up near The Two Spindoctors pub last week."

That perked Rodney up no end. He was such a sucker for birds. Birds and football. Luke phoned Frederick – just three pips as they'd agreed at school – and fifteen minutes later the silkily skilful sweeper rang the front doorbell.

"It's Frederick Dulac, Mum," Luke said brightly. "He's found some barn owls to show me and Rodney. Up near the Heights. We'll only be an hour."

"You're in Luke's class, aren't you?" his mum asked, with her usual welcoming scowl. "Do *you* do this Extra Biology that Luke's started going to?"

"It's really wicked," Frederick said. "Fast-track education. It *kicks*."

She looked at him oddly. She couldn't bear the way he spoke, but she knew he was a top student. "So will you be going this Saturday afternoon too?"

He widened his eyes. "No way I'd miss it!"

"Oh, go on with you then. Go and gawp at your owls."

"I don't *like* misleading your mother like this," Rodney sighed on the ride up to the Heights. "And she's not stupid. I don't think she's buying 'Extra Biology' for a minute. I know I wouldn't. What sort of teachers would go back and give *more* lessons during a half-term holiday? They'd have to be ... morons."

Luke and Frederick just looked at each other. They rested their case.

You couldn't actually see James Prince's mansion from the road. Just a massive pair of wrought-iron gates, then what looked like a small forest. Luke grinned. A kid no older than him and Frederick lived here. And the word was, he hardly ever came out. His mum and dad were now on his own Majestic Software payroll, along with a butler, cook, chauffeur, gardener, you name it. A private tutor was helicoptered in from Cambridge to make sure he got a *real* fast-track education. But most of the time he just sat in front of a screen, changing the face of modern computing, raking in more dosh in a week than Castle Albion had made in their whole inglorious history.

"That's a thought!" Luke said suddenly as Frederick buzzed the intercom and gave his name and business. "This kid could *buy* the Albion, inject masses of new cash and build a brand new stadium. They say he's football crazy, right?"

"Well there's a club badge on this intercom," said Frederick, peering closer.

"*Albion's?*" Even Rodney was getting excited now.

"Oh get real," Frederick told him. "A kid this rich? Never leaves the house. Only ever watches football on the box. Who's *he* gonna support?"

"Man U," Luke and Rodney groaned in chorus. It was all so predictable.

Two men were coming out of the forest. Marching in step like soldiers. Big guys. Humping great security types with muscles on their muscles. They were dressed in black penguin suits, bright white shirts and black bow-ties. But both were wearing armbands. When they were close enough, Luke saw beautifully embroidered Red Devil logos on them. To the right was stitched JPMS – James Prince Majestic Software; to the left MUFC – Massively Unavoidable Football Contagion (or words to that effect).

"You've brought the items?" asked Penguin One, while still strutting.

"No sweat," smiled Frederick, showing his bag that held fifteen vinyl singles.

"Is 'All Kinds of Everything' by Dana in this batch?" asked Penguin Two. "Mr Prince was particularly hopeful of enjoying that one in his jacuzzi tonight."

"Expecting it on Friday. Israeli import. Friday – on my life."

"Can we – er – come in, then?" Rodney asked. It was starting to rain again.

"No need," said Penguin One. Instead he buzzed the gate back a bit, snatched Frederick's bag, and slammed it shut again. "OK," he said into a small mike. Then he added, after adjusting his earpiece: "Mr Prince's secretary has now transferred the first instalment of the fee into your bank account, Mr Dulac."

"Hey," Penguin Two smiled. "You're *Frederick* Dulac, right? And *you're* the Studless Sensation! No kiddin'!" He dipped his hands into his pockets and came up with a biro and an old Laser Quest scoresheet. He passed them through the gates. "Just sign your names, lads. It's for my – um – little girl."

"What's she called?" asked Luke, pen poised.

"Oh . . . ah . . . Bryan-y! That's it! *Bryany!* But if you could just put 'To Bryan', she'd love it." Even in the dark he'd gone as red as a Man U shirt. "Cheers."

Frederick signed too and passed the pen and paper back. "Cheers then – Bryan."

Penguin Two just smiled sheepishly. Then Penguin One waddled in. "Anyway lads," he said, "at least you're on the right side: playing *with* Chopper Foggon."

"Sorry?"

"Well, you wouldn't want to enter *that* old boy's aggravation zone! We're ex-CID, both of us, and we get to hear things – you get my drift? Misbehaviour *off* the field as well as on it. One time Chopper got his own back on this bloke who'd scratched his car bumper. Just a little nick it was, but he completely lost it. Dragged the guy back to his place and gave him the third degree with this four-foot bit of scaffolding, a bottle of Jif, a Bunsen burner and . . ."

"Nah, that's eighteen-certificate stuff," Penguin Two cut in. "Good luck Saturday, lads. See you." And they turned and marched off into the depths of the forest.

"Right," said Rodney, rubbing his hands. "Where did you hear that owl?"

18

Benny Webb had something special up his sleeve for training on Wednesday. After the fiasco against Rotherham and with Newcastle up ahead on Saturday, everyone expected a gruelling morning. If no one died of exhaustion, they must have been cheating – *that* sort of session.

But out on the centre spot Benny greeted his boys with a broad grin. There were no cones to race round. No markers to show the limits of the areas they had to practise moves in (and *keep on* practising till they got them right). Most amazing of all, the pitch wasn't littered with ancient footballs. There was just the one. A brand-spanking-new white affair. And Benny was juggling with it – happy as a sandboy. Foot to foot. Foot to knee. Knee to head. Head into hands.

"Right lads!" he beamed. "Welcome to Ash Acre! I hope you have a really great time today!" He paused for what seemed like an age.

"*That's* the message we've got to give to our fans on Saturday!"

"He's boozed up," murmured Narris behind Luke. "Look how red his face is."

"He's been at the pre-match hip-flask," Chrissie Pick agreed. "I can smell it."

"Now look," Benny was rattling on. "We've had our ups and downs over the past couple of weeks. More downs than ups, if you wanna get technical about it. But we can't let that get to us. First and foremost, football is an expression of pure *joy*. Man has never come up with a better way to celebrate the sheer delight of bein' alive. Every time a sleek, well-honed professional athlete puts foot to ball, he is striking a blow for the beauty of all civilization. Every time he heads it, he's soundin' a note in the sweetest human symphony..."

"He can count *me* out of this," grunted Dennis Meldrum. "All I ever do is shut down wingers and take the odd throw-in."

"D'you think he's flipped?" asked Half-Fat, not altogether joking. "Should we get a stretcher and tie him down?"

"There is no *point* in playing football unless every moment is a form of ecstasy. Unless you *love* every second that you're out on that pitch. You owe it to yourself. You owe it to your fans. And you owe it to Him Up In The Heavens who created this most magnificent of all sports in the first place." He paused to go eyeball-to-eyeball with the entire squad – each member of which fully expected him to start frothing at the mouth. "So that is why this mornin' you will not *train*, but you will play. Just play – with this lovely ball here – to your heart's content. Play a beautiful game of football. And then go home."

A cheer went up. Madman threw in a snatch of Tiger Moth sounds. Luke smiled at Frederick. So that was it. Benny wanted them to go Back To Basics. Rediscover The Fun Of Football. And for the next hour that was pretty much what they did. But they all knew what they were playing for. A place in the side for the plum tie against Newcastle. No one could bear to think of missing out on that one.

They picked sides like kids in a park. Gaffer Mann and Ruel were skippers. Chopper got picked first, just in case he cut up rough. Luke and Frederick wound up on the same side, and they played their socks off – in Luke's case, his trainers too. If Benny had noticed he wasn't wearing boots, he didn't say a word. In fact Benny didn't say very much at all.

He just stayed on the centre spot, watching the game ebb and flow around him. Mostly he smiled. There was plenty to smile about. If just half the team had played like this at Rotherham, they'd have cruised it. If all of them managed it against Newcastle on Saturday, they just might be in with a prayer. Confident, snappy, s*mart* football. At last Benny's Dream seemed to be coming true.

Amazingly enough, even Chopper wasn't having a mare. He must have known this was a trip to the Last Chance Saloon for him. Just as Benny seemed a little more *mellow* than usual, so Chopper seemed almost gentle, swearing on average only three times a minute, helping up players he'd floored, making sure that when he spat it missed an opponent. Once or twice he even managed to find a team-mate with a pass. But however little damage he did, he couldn't hold a candle to the towering defensive partnership that Frederick and Gaffer Mann had struck up. Now there *was* a telepathic understanding. It was as if they'd been playing together for longer than Jimmy Hill had been shaving.

When Benny blew the final whistle, it was as if a huge cloud had lifted from Ash Acre stadium. You couldn't move for chuffed smiles and slapped backs all round. "Your mate and Gaffer," Craig Edwards panted at Luke, "they're like Campbell and Adams. It's got to be the axe for Chopper now."

"Yeah," said Half-Fat, "but has Benny got the bottle to do it?"

"*Bottle?* Hip-flask, more like," Carl suggested. "That must be why he got bladdered. Look, he's calling Chopper over. *I do believe he's gonna do it!"*

The cloud that had cleared over Ash Acre suddenly loomed again. It seemed to squirt up into the sky directly out of the narrowed eyes of the Man Who Loved Walls. Everyone else stopped and watched him stamp into the centre circle. This would be something to tell their grandchildren about, and besides, some of them might need to rush up and put Benny back together again afterwards.

This was how Benny always told a player he "wouldn't be involved" in the next game. Summons to the centre spot. Arm around the shoulder. There went the arm now. But this was no usual "resting" of a first-team squad member.

Chopper Foggon had made two hundred and sixty-nine consecutive starts for the Albion. (OK, he'd been suspended for thirty-seven games along the way but that didn't count.) For six lethal seasons he'd been first name on the teamsheet, if only because Benny had never dared to put him second. He was as much a part of the Castle Albion scenery as the tannoy that didn't work and the stink of ghastly-burgers. And now – four days from Albion's biggest *ever* game – his head was on the block.

Luke knew he wasn't alone in closing his eyes as Benny said the words into the hard man's ear. Scaffolding, Jif, Bunsen burner ... he thought, shivering. (What *did* he do with that Bunsen burner?) Maybe all the king's horses and all the king's men wouldn't be able to mend old Benny after Chopper's response.

But when he looked again, he blinked. Chopper was shaking Benny's hand! He was smiling a weird, it's-a-fair-cop kind of smile! Then he just trotted off down the tunnel. Benny could hardly believe it either. He snatched out his hip-flask and took a big swig. Then he grinned at all the others and held up his thumb. It was done and dusted. *There* went *the Chopper!* A curtain came down on an era.

But why hadn't Chopper gone mental? Luke didn't like it. It didn't feel *right*.

19

Thursday was the last day before half-term. After training on Wednesday Luke had had to rush back for PSE so he hadn't had a chance to chat with Frederick about the new Chopper situation. But Frederick had said he would be at school on Thursday. They could talk then – but hey, what was there to talk about?

Plenty, thought Luke. And the longer Thursday went on, the more worried he got. Chopper's reaction had just been too … unChopper-like. After clattering Gaffer Mann and then trying to shop Frederick to the press – all just to keep his place in the team – why was he then so calm when Benny dropped him? There was something going on. Something iffy. Scaffolding, Jif, Bunsen burner…

Frederick didn't show for any of the regular lessons. No change there, then. But Luke dashed out of his last lesson right on the bell to make sure he caught his mate on his way in. He waited at the gates for ten minutes. His mum must have been held up by a vital cream-cake purchasing decision in her favourite café. So he got to wait another ten minutes too. But still no sign of Frederick.

Grisly thoughts kept creeping into Luke's mind. If Frederick said he would be somewhere, he meant it. That way, he was as reliable as Michael Owen in front of an open goal. So where was he? Right from the start of all this, Luke had felt protective towards his mate. However cool the guy was, he felt responsible for him. It was Luke, after all, who had got him involved with the Albion in the first place. Grisly thoughts, grisly thoughts... And then as if all the dark shapes in his head had taken on a human form, up came Mr Bates.

"All set for the holiday, then?" Bates asked almost affectionately. "Gonna be doing anythin' interesting?" What was going on here? First Chopper, now the Caretaker From Hell – bad guys weren't meant to *be* like this.

"Well, um," Luke stammered, not quite sure how to have a regular conversation with a bloke who was usually threatening to slap you with a mop. "There's the big game on Saturday."

Briefly Mr Bates looked confused. It was probably hard for him to think as far as two days ahead. If he'd been any closer, Luke might have heard the cogs and chains of his brain clanking.

"Newcastle!" he grinned at last. "Proud

Newcastle. The high-flying Magpies. Oh, they're passionate about their football up in Geordie-land." Like most modern armchair fans, he was stuffed to the gills with words of wisdom that he'd picked up off the telly. Then he frowned. Lots more clanking upstairs. This was obviously going to be an industrial-strength cliché. "Although since the mid-fifties they've won surprisingly little silverware – wouldn't you say?"

"Yeah, right," said Luke with a frown of his own, looking out for Frederick.

"But I still reckon you'll do 'em," Mr Bates called over his shoulder as he walked away. "No problem. I reckon you're gonna 'ave 'em. You've got to field the right team, that's all. The right blend of youth and experience."

"Cheers," said Luke, not really listening. He had too much else on his mind. Still Frederick hadn't shown. And now his mum was bringing the Escort to a halt twenty yards up the street. She wasn't a Premier League parker. If she stopped within two car-lengths of you, that was a good result. Luke went across, she overshot, he backtracked, got in – and went home for half-term.

As usual, the break from school started up less brilliantly than he'd been expecting. Luke lived for the holidays but as soon as they began he always remembered how boring they were. As per usual too, his mum gave him a list of chores for the week. Not just tidying his room and doing a bit of shopping. He had to uproot a minor forest at the bottom of the garden and chop it all for firewood. Nothing is certain in football, but Luke had a pretty fair idea that David Beckham didn't prepare for crucial Cup-ties by tearing up trees.

It was early on Friday evening, while he was making a bonfire of the smaller branches, that his mum came stomping down the garden path.

"Someone's on the phone for you," she shouted. From her tone, she could have been announcing a terrorist outrage in the sitting room.

"It – it's not a Mr Mallard, is it?" asked Luke, shrinking.

"No. It's *a girl*!"

Baffled, Luke followed her into the house. His mum's back looked furious. *Gardens for Gastronomes* was on in half an hour, and she hated to be disturbed during her pre-programme build-up.

"Hi, Luke? Oh look, this is Adele – Frederick's sister? Hate to bother you."

"Bother away," Luke replied. *A girl*, his mum had said. And what a girl. (Adele Dulac could have been a supermodel, no question. She made Naomi Campbell look like Lenny Henry in a fright wig. Instead she'd chosen to train as a barrister. One day soon, some very lucky villains were going to find her fighting their corner in court. Maybe crime *did* pay, after all.)

"You don't happen to know where Frederick is, do you, Luke? Only a stretch limo has just pulled up outside and the chauffeur's waiting for a single – 'All Kinds of Everything' by Dana? For a Mr Prince?"

"Yeah, I know about that. Frederick did say he'd have it by today. But no, I haven't seen him since Wednesday."

"Nor me. Oh well. He'll show up. He always does."

"But... But... Aren't you worried? Shouldn't *we* be worried? I mean..."

"Hey, Studless Sensation, chill out! Frederick's been gone for way longer than this before. He's cool. And then there's your big game tomorrow. He's hardly likely to miss out on *that*, now is he?"

I wonder, thought Luke as he put down the phone. I wonder.

At four minutes past two precisely, on Saturday February the nineteenth, it all went pear-shaped for Luke. It had been fairly Kiwi-fruit-shaped up till then as well. Twice he'd rung Adele to see if Frederick was back. Twice she'd laughed and said no – but that one day Luke would make someone a wonderful mother.

Luke was more concerned about his own mum. On most football days she went on red alert, but this was something else. She wouldn't let him out of her sight for a second. He couldn't even get Rodney alone to ask if they should tell the police that Cool F had lost all his markers. And the *looks* she kept giving him!

"So have you got all your books ready for Extra Biology?" she asked Luke across the kitchen table as Rodney finished washing up. It was three minutes past two.

"All taken care of, dear," Rodney said over his shoulder. "His bag's in the Escort." He had the lucky pink pinny on – and wouldn't be taking it off till the final whistle at four forty-five. "I'll run him up to school now. Before I do the shopping."

"That won't be necessary," Luke's mum said in a bizarre sing-song voice. "*I'll* take Luke to ... Extra Biology."

Luke was struck dumb.

"But... But..." Rodney stuttered, swinging round.

"No buts!" she declared, raising a hand for silence. "*I'll* take him. Then *you* can shop. Put your skates on then, Luke. Don't you have to be there for two-fifteen?"

There was absolutely nothing Luke or Rodney could do. When she was this determined, even the combined persuasive powers of the *Reservoir Dogs* couldn't have made her change her mind. Luke stood up, shared a look of deep despair with Rodney, then trudged out to the Escort.

His mum was beside him in an instant, gunning up the engine, getting it to fire after only three tries. (Why did cars never clap out when you wanted them to?) As soon as she saw that his school was all locked up, she would go ballistic. There was no way back for Luke now. He'd walked out on to Ash Acre's sacred turf for the last time. If his mum played true to form, he might never walk again at all. Already he could hear that nutty humming noise she made when she was winding herself up for a wobbler. This, surely, was as bad as it got?

But no – there was worse! A single glance in the wing mirror piled on the horror. They were being followed. A flashy silver-grey BMW. A driver in Raybans, with sticking plasters on his forehead and cheek, a wad of papers poking out of his Boss suit-jacket pocket. Neil Veal was back on the case!

Luke sank lower in the seat and closed his eyes. He opened them only when the car juddered to a halt. They were outside the school gates – as locked as the door to the Crown Jewels, but with those same spiky railings that they used to plonk traitors' heads on. Agent Veal had taxied to a halt ten yards behind.

"No," Luke said before his mum's humming started to make the car shake. "Not here. The back entrance. We've got to go in at the back."

She didn't look too impressed by that. But she gunned up the Escort again. She could put her wobbler on hold for a few moments more. Off they went. On came Neil Veal in pursuit. He seemed to be mouthing the words "Third party?"

The back gate was smaller than the front and to Luke's huge surprise it was ajar. He noticed this as his pitiful parker of a mum overshot it before pulling up outside the caretaker's house, just behind Mr Bates's van. Luke twisted round to see the agent stop thankfully *short* of the gate. And just at that moment Mr Bates himself emerged from the school. He bent to put down a tray on the pavement, then turned to shut and start locking the gate again.

Luke had to move fast – and he did. "Right Mum, thanks for the lift," he cried, leaping out of the car. "See you just after five. Have a good afternoon." Her jaw had dropped. Out on the street Luke could still hear her humming. But he'd seen a glimmer of hope. He turned his eyes to the back entrance. Everything now depended on getting that Crazy Caretaker to let him in. Everything. "Mr Bates," he called out with a huge forced grin, walking briskly up to him.

It was only a matter of twelve steps or so. It took Luke five seconds, tops. But an awful lot happened before he got to the gate – most of it inside Luke's whirring brain. First Mr Bates looked his way in sheer panic. Then he stopped fiddling with the lock, pushed back the gate and nudged the tray back in with his foot – supposedly out of sight. But Mr Bates never did anything right.

Behind him, Luke clearly saw the leftovers of somebody's lunch. A vile-looking school-type lunch. Bit of a gutted Cornish pastie, burnt chips, baked beans in globby sauce. But next to it was a sherbet dip – its stick of liquorice taken out and laid alongside it. *Somebody's* lunch. Somebody *in* the school at that very moment. Somebody who perhaps wasn't *meant* to be there...

"What do you want, nipper?" Mr Bates barked, still looking petrified.

Nipper. That's what struck the match in Luke's head. "We'll 'ave you, nipper... We're gonna 'ave you..." That disguised but familiar voice on Frederick's phone – it had been Mr Bates! Chopper's mate. Chopper's hanger-on. He'd do anything for Chopper. Including keeping a far better player under wraps just so Chopper could be in the team. It had to be! That van up by his house – it was the one Luke had seen outside Frederick's. This dumb prat had snatched Luke's mate and locked him up in the school! He'd put the "kid" back into "kidnapping" and now it was up to Luke to set Frederick free.

Right away a plan of action began to form in his head, first of all he had to win the idiot's trust.

"It's OK," he whispered, "Chopper sent me."

"*Chopper!* Why?" Just the name made Bates jump. "Has the plan changed?"

You could say that, thought Luke. "Let me in and I'll tell you."

Mr Bates couldn't shift quick enough. He shoved back the gate and went inside, putting

116

his foot slap-bang in the plate of stodge. As he bent to curse and clean his sole, Luke followed him in, then took a step back and turned. Smiling happily, he waved to his defeated mum and blew her a kiss. She'd seen him go in: she'd put him on the spot and he'd come up trumps. Wobbler Postponed.

Off she drove, jaw clenched, eyes fixed to the front – which meant she didn't see Agent Veal revving up his BMW ready to continue the chase. But Luke quickly waved at him to stop. He wanted Veal with *him* – as back-up. He reckoned it would be easy enough to trick Bates into taking him to Cool F. But then he might need a bit of extra muscle to help to get him out. He waved harder.

Vealy noticed and switched off his engine, looking puzzled. Luke grinned, pointed over his shoulder at Bates then held up three fingers.

"Third party!" Veal mouthed in delight – and he was out of that Ultimate Driving Machine like a shot. Luke put a finger to his lips as if it was all a bit of a game, beckoned him on, and slipped back inside the school gate.

21

"So what's up?" Mr Bates grunted, scuffing the last of the beans off his shoe. "How come you're with the Chopper now? Why'd he send you? I done everything just like he told me. I ain't done nothin' wrong. You saying I done it wrong, *nipper*?"

He took a menacing, sauce-stained step towards Luke. It didn't take much to get old Batesy cooking. He liked to get his retaliation in first. So he was just as likely to smack Luke around a bit *before* getting answers to his questions. Luke knew he had to keep him confused, but just on the right side of violence. He also had to stop him from seeing Neil Veal creeping in behind.

"No, Chopper's well chuffed with you," Luke said, daring to take Mr Bates's arm, turning him away from the gate and leading him on down to the first block of buildings. "Well chuffed. He really wanted you to know that."

That put a spring back in his step. "So what did he send you for?"

Before answering, Luke snatched a look back over his shoulder. Agent Veal had prowled in behind them. In one hand he held the New Client contract he wanted signed on Luke's behalf. Again Luke put a finger to his lips. Veal did the same back, then held up three fingers. "Third party," he mouthed, nodding knowingly at Bates. This Agent knew as well as any slide-tackler that timing is crucial – so he would wait for *just* the right moment to introduce himself.

"Why did Chopper send you?" Mr Bates said again, more brutal than before, but also in a lower voice. Not much more than a hiss. Already it was weird enough being in school without all the usual din. Luke's ears pricked up.

"Why are we whispering?" he whispered, as they approached the great brick wall of the boiler room. *Fart if you hate the Arsenal!* had been aerosoled on it.

"Well he'll hear us, won't he, you lemon!" growled Bates, pointing down a mossy flight of outside steps to a small basement door. "Then he'll *know*."

"Ah – right." Luke nodded, then paused. "Know ... what?"

"*That it's us who nabbed him!*" Bates was almost dancing on the spot with the effort of keeping his voice down and his excitement in.

119

"With that blindfold on, he dunno where he is or who put 'im there. But as soon as he recognizes our voices, it'll blow our cover. He'll know who we are. And you know what that would mean?" His face darkened. "Then we'd have to take him *right* out."

"Take him out," Luke repeated, eyes widening. Pole, Jif, Bunsen burner...

"Snuff him," Bates added, just for the sake of clarity. "*Retire* him."

They were at the top of the steps. Glancing back, Luke saw Veal by a wheelie-bin – checking the contract papers and getting ready for a man-to-man exchange with the guy he thought Luke's mum had hired as her hardnut negotiator.

"So what's the rap, then?" Bates wheezed. "I done it all – snatched 'im, trussed 'im up, got the blindfold on, got 'im his meals on time. Even went out and got 'im some *sherbet*! Don't Chopper trust me all of a sudden?"

"No, no! I mean yes! Whatever. Chopper's sure you've got it spot on..."

"'Cos I've done it by the flippin' book, I have," he hissed. "I could *show* you what a crackin' job I made of it. I could show you, *nipper*!"

"Yeah!" Luke exclaimed. "Show me. That's it! Show me how it's done. *That*'s why Chopper sent me: so I could learn from a real *master*!"

But the Crackpot Caretaker had got himself

into a state. He didn't just go down the greasy steps and ask Luke to follow. He grabbed the boy by the scruff of his neck and pretty well carried him down. Luke's feet were still off the ground as Batesy reached for his bunch of keys and thrust one into the lock. "Show you...!" he kept muttering. "I'll *show* you! I'll show anyone who flippin' wants to look!"

The door sprang back a little way, then Bates kicked it wide open. And in that split second, Luke got sloppy. "Frederick!" he cried, loud enough to wake every sleeping giant in the lower reaches of the Nationwide League.

"Hey Luke, 'nuff respect," grinned Frederick from the concrete pillar he stood lashed to. So much for Batesy's kidnap-masterclass: Cool F had already eased off his blindfold by rubbing the back of his head against the pillar.

Luke heard a deep, deep groan come from the guy who was holding him. But before Bates could think of "retiring" Frederick, a voice out-side distracted him.

"Hi there!" floated down from the top of the steps. Reeling now, Bates swivelled round. "This seems to me like a pretty good time to set the ball rolling," the voice went on. "Veal's the name. Neil Veal – celebrity agent: *'The Cash Is Out There. All I Ask Is Ten Per Cent...'* Ha-ha..."

He came down the steps into view – and handed the gaping Bates a sheet of paper. "But seriously, I *can* be flexible on commission in certain areas. Take a look, I've printed up a list of them – book deals, video tie-ins, that kind of thing – so if you'd *just* care to cast your eyes..."

Then his mobile warbled. With a flourish he whipped it out. "Bear with me," he grinned, turning away and shooting back the aerial – right up into Big Batesy's eye. That woke up the Kidnap King good and proper. "You glopper!" he growled, smacking Veal hard on the back of the head. First the phone hit the deck, then the agent. Then Bates dived down on top of him, fists still flying.

Incredibly, Veal kept on talking through the pummelling: "Well maybe, yes – *Oof!* – I *could* go lower on after-dinner speaking... *Aaagh!* Eight and a half per cent on cereal-packet toys: I can't say fairer than that... *Uurghhh!*"

But with Bates otherwise occupied he'd let go of Luke, who rushed across and started undoing Cool F's knots. They weren't all that tight. Within moments Frederick was freed up enough to help Luke to loosen the rest. "Rockin' idea," he smiled, "bringing Veal as the decoy!" Double-quick they got to the last knot. Frederick stepped over the rope and gave Luke a little bow.

Behind them the agent had stopped rabbiting on. And there were now fewer *Aaagh*s and *Uurghhh*s as well. The boys turned to find Bates lying half-in, half-out of the basement room. And Vealy – having finally wised up to the fact that Bates *wasn't* just playing the tough negotiator – was sitting across his chest and pinning down both arms with his knees. Even so, the useless Bates was still desperately trying to knock seven shades of brown sugar out of him.

Well in control, however, the agent picked his mobile off the floor, called 999, and told the police that he would very much like to see them at their earliest convenience. Then he grinned at Castle Albion's two brightest young stars. "Hey you," he cried. "Get outta here! You've got a Cup-tie to win!"

"Are you sure?" asked Luke. "Can you hang on till the police come?"

The agent nodded at the handbag hardnut thrashing beneath him and snorted.

Masterful or what? Fair play to the guy – he'd shown a whole crateful of bottle here. "Just make those Geordies weep!" he told Luke and Frederick as they passed. "Then let's do post-match bubbly!"

22

Luke and Frederick had to run all the way to Ash Acre. There was no chance of getting there any quicker on wheels. All the roads round the ground were gridlocked with matchday traffic, even though there were only twenty minutes to kick-off. Little Castle Albion just didn't seem geared up for the big time. What they needed was an easy-access, 25,000 seater, purpose-built stadium on the outskirts of town with an enormous, efficiently-run car-park. *Dream on!*

As they got closer, lots of people recognized them. Mini Metros bulging with teenaged blokes. Tiny kids marching along holding their dads' hands. Old boys with walking sticks leaning on the front gates of their little houses. All of them waved and cheered as Luke and Frederick raced by. "You'll do it, lads!" "One-nil to the Albion!" "You're on your way to Wembley!" "Shove it up those Geordie back-sides!" FA Cup fever – in spades. And Luke was catching the bug. *What if...? What if...? What if...?* he kept thinking to the rhythm of his running. What if they *did* just pull it off out there on the park against the Magpies? What dancing there would be in the streets around Castle Albion then!

At two fifty-one they battled their way through the ticket queues and stumbled into Ash Acre. They'd missed the pre-match warm-up. With a bit of luck, they'd have missed Benny Webb's pre-match briefing too. But there was precious little time to get changed. The club staff knew that too. As soon as they caught sight of Luke and Frederick, massive smiles lit up their faces. Then they rushed to pull back doors, clear corridors and get them down to Benny and the boys pronto.

But just as they were tearing past the Away Team dressing room, the door opened and a big guy poked out his head. Big in every sense. In fact, as far as Luke was concerned, they didn't come any bigger. Haarlem, Feyenoord and PSV Eindhoven in Holland; AC Milan and Sampdoria in Italy; and then finally, unforgettably, Chelsea in England – all these clubs had been bejewelled by the sexy soccer skills of this most cultured colossus. Big in skill, big in spirit, big in hair certainly – there really was Only One Ruud Gullit: now manager of Newcastle United but worshipped the whole world over. Big, Big, BIG!

"Hey boys!" he said, in his unmistakable accent, as Luke skidded to an awestruck halt. "The heating's gone off in our dressing room again. It's freezing in here. Can't somebody fix it? It's really ... sloppy."

Then he pulled his head back in, dreadlocks in a right twist. But as Luke and Frederick grinned at each other, out it popped again. "Oh yeah," he added with just a faint smile, "and have a good game, you two. But not *too* good, right?"

"You bet!" laughed Luke.

"Happenin'," agreed Cool Frederick. Then they sped on towards the scuffed blue door marked *Home Team*. But before they burst in, Frederick turned to Luke. "Hey," he said. "I owe you for getting me out. But let's just focus on the game now, yeah? Forget about Foggon."

"Whatever you say," Luke nodded. But Chopper would have to answer for himself afterwards – him and Batesy, both. You could take the men out of the prison, as Vealo said, but you could stick them right back in there too.

The welcome they got in their own stuffy dressing room took the roof off. The sheer din must have blown a fresh blast of cold air over the Newcastle lot huddling in next door. For half a minute it was like the goal celebration pile-up to end all goal celebration pile-ups. Then from under the ruck, Luke felt a hand in a sheep-skinned sleeve dragging him out and turning him towards his peg.

"Stone me, Luke," he sighed. "You cut it a bit fine, didn't you?" Then he reached in and pulled out Cool F. "You too, Frederick. Now get your kits on – sharpish! And the rest of you lot – *siddown*!"

One person was already sitting down. One person hadn't moved a muscle since Luke and Frederick's entrance. No, there had been half an inch of movement. That was the distance his great stubbly jaw had dropped when Frederick charged in.

"Chopper, me old mate," Benny said, turning to this utterly gobsmacked person, "Looks like I won't be needing you in the starting line-up after all. Get a tracksuit on. You're back on the bench with the trainees."

Luke, changing fast, had his back to the hard man. He couldn't see the look on his face now, couldn't see how he was eyeballing Frederick – but he had a pretty fair idea. "Thank Gawd you two got here, Luke," Terry the Physio said under his breath. "With Chopper in, we'd have got hammered."

"Cheers," said Luke. "Oh, Ruud Gullit said the heating's gone off next door."

"I should flippin' well hope it has! Premier League nancy boys!" He winked and nudged

Luke in the ribs. "It'll probably be on the blink at half-time too."

Then there was a soft, low moan from the floor. Luke spun round, afraid that Chopper might have decked Benny or even Frederick. But it was Carl Davey.

"Get up Carl, will you," snapped Benny. "What you makin' that noise for?"

The Striker With The Thing About Pineapples was sitting on the tiles, rubbing his thigh, and wincing in agony. "It's no good, Boss," he howled. "I've done meself in. Jumping up when the lads got here. I must've pulled a muscle."

Terry swooped down next to him and prodded his leg. Carl's language then could *not* have been broadcast before the nine o'clock watershed. "There's no way he'll play today, Boss," was Terry's verdict. "You big girl's blouse, Carl!"

"Right, right..." Benny thought out loud as he went into a brand new spin. "Kick-off in four minutes... Can't throw a trainee in – too much pressure..." He turned to the last bloke everyone else would have considered. "Chopper."

"Yeah, Boss?" He still hadn't got a sub's tracksuit on. He didn't look capable.

"I'm playing you as an emergency second striker, up with Ruel."

A murmur of disbelief filled the room. Chopper! Up front? He usually crossed the halfway line about four times a season. To him, a shot was a jab you got in the arm before you went abroad. And the last time he'd actually scored, England were still fancying their chances in penalty shoot-outs. But now it was up to him to hit the net like ritual-mad Carl Davey. No one spoke. Then Craig Edwards looked down at the pineapple that was already in his hands.

"Don't ... Even ... *Think* ... About It!" snarled Chopper, suddenly back on song.

"Right lads, get out there!" Benny roared. "And I wanna see you with your *Cup* heads on today! No more Scarboroughs or Rotherhams. Be cool! Be *smart*!"

23

As soon as Castle Albion's chosen few took the field, the hardcore fans packing the South Side spotted something different. Or rather, their leader Rocky Mitford did. You had to get up pretty early in the morning to catch *him* out. Straightaway Rocky's foghorn voice blared out across the pitch:

"Give us an S!" he bellowed.

"S!" the 5,000 around him obediently bellowed back.

"Give us a T!"

"T!"

"Give us a U!"

"U!"

"And give us a D!"

"D!"

"And let's have an L!"

"L!"

"Oh, for cryin' out loud!" Rocky boomed. "This is gonna take all day – but you know where we're goin'. So tell me: what have you got in the end?"

"THE STUDLESS SENSATION!"

And they were right. Luke had trotted out in his trainers. He raised an arm to the Albion faithful. If he had a stinker today, it wouldn't be his footwear's fault.

But Luke wasn't thinking stinker. Nor was Milkesy thinking *he* might go sour, nor Phizzo that he might go flat. Because here they were inside a packed Ash Acre – no snow, no rain, (no programmes for most of the fans, but Albion *never* printed enough). And this was nothing less than the fifth round of the world's oldest cup competition, with John Motson up in the TV gantry, Newcastle United kicking in at the other end – and a place in the last eight at stake. OK, so the tannoy had already packed in. But if you couldn't lift yourself for a fixture like this, you had to weigh ten tons!

Luke felt pure adrenaline gush through his veins. And from the panther-like way Frederick moved as he gave Madman some easy catches, *he* could have focused for England. The fans saw how up-for-it he was.

"You're Cool And You Know You Are!"

they sang at full throttle, over and over, until he nodded their way. For that, they gave him a quick respectful burst of "I Should Be So Lucky". And then, almost before Luke was ready, Gaffer had won the toss, Ruel kicked off, and Chopper – standing right up alongside him – took the pass.

It was perhaps only then that *everyone* in the stadium realized that Foggon, C, was on the team sheet as a striker. It seemed to dawn on Chopper himself too. He stared at the ball as if it were a bunch of flowers. People didn't usually *pass* it to him. The only time he ever touched it was when it rolled his way and he hoofed it into touch or upfield. But *he* was the furthest man forward now.

Looking like he was about to have a nose-bleed, he seized up completely. His opposite number in the Newcastle shirt couldn't believe his luck. Darting forward he nicked the ball off Chopper's foot, rounded him and rocketed off into Albion territory. Normally this wouldn't have been a total disaster. There were still, after all, ten more Albion men between striker and goal. But this wasn't just any old number nine. This was the captain of England. The priciest goal-machine in British transfer history. This was Alan Super-Shearer!

Now Shearer's not especially fast. Sharp as a razor in the six-yard box, heck of a shot on him outside it, brilliant in the air, fit as fifteen fiddles – but not *that* quick. So no one could explain afterwards how he managed to outpace every single Albion outfielder. Maybe they were all too stunned by Chopper's give-away in the centre circle. But Shearer just left them all for dead. And when Madman dashed out to close him down, he rifled the ball right past him and that was that.

The Magpie fans at the Town End broke the sound barrier. One-nil up and half the Toon Army hadn't even breathed out since the starting whistle. Albion caught cold? They could have been walled up inside eleven individual igloos!

Ruel kicked off again, but this time Luke stood next to him, received the pass and slid it back to Half-Fat. Frederick loped forward, took the ball in his stride then sprayed it wide to Chrissie. Three passes later Ruel had a clear header on goal, which Shay Given gathered at a bit of a stretch. Now Albion (and their shell-shocked fans) were back at the races. If only the game had started at one minute past three.

After those first few disastrous seconds, Albion soon looked more Premier League-ish than the visitors. Cool Frederick didn't let Shearer get another sniff, while bootless Luke ran the show in midfield – leaving Robert Lee chasing shadows and tying their defence in knots with a stream of stonking through-balls. But wouldn't you know it – the guy on the end of every Albion attack was Chopper Foggon. And the great lump kept rounding them off with handbag shots, handbag headers and some really quite superb air-kicks.

As half-time approached – and Chopper sent

yet another Chrissie cross into the crowd near the corner flag – Luke could just imagine what Trevor Brooking would be telling the nation when they showed the game's highlights later that night on *Match of the Day*. "We-e-e-ll," he'd say, "You *did* begin to get the feeling that this *just* might not be Castle Albion's day. You started to wonder whether *any* of those very good chances *were* going to go in..."

Then suddenly it wasn't Shay Given's goal that everyone was looking at – but Madman's. In a rare upfield sortie Robert Lee managed to take the ball past Narris and went for goal. Gaffer lunged in, clipped Lee's ankle, down he went just inside the box – penalty!

Only one man was going to take this. Up stepped Alan the Assassin. Shearer was about to strike again – and he never missed from the spot. Even while your Southgates and your Battys and your Inces were fouling up in the semi-finals of major tournaments, this guy could always be relied on to stick his pens away.

But then again, thought Luke, as Rocky and the South Siders kicked up a storm of boos and hisses to put him off, he didn't have to beat Madman Mort every week. Argie and German keepers were one thing. This Nationwide Nutter was quite another. And as if to prove the point, Madman flicked up his goalie's top to give the Geordie God a quick flash of the black-and-white latex skeleton chest that he was wearing underneath!

Shearer didn't even blink. Nothing could distract him from the thing he loved doing most: hitting the back of the net. In he pounded. Luke could hardly look. Madman himself seemed to be flinching. Shearer gave the ball an almighty wallop – high to Madman's right. But Gordon Banks and Peter Shilton – who were they? Madman didn't just *save* it at full stretch. He *caught* it!

The half-time whistle went as the kooky keeper rushed to the North Stand to celebrate. Luke raced after to hug him. But as he did so, a flash of dark blue with bits of silver caught his eye near the tunnel. Several flashes. Serious-looking uniforms. Police uniforms – and alongside them: Vealy. Winking.

24

The police wanted to nab Chopper then and there. One of them even had a pair of handcuffs ready. But Benny wasn't having any of that. He shooed them and Neil V back into the bowels of Ash Acre – clearing a path for *all* the players (including Chopper) to troop down the tunnel and into the dressing room.

Luke was the last one in. The flush-faced, Elastoplastered Veal was scribbling new figures on to a wad of forms. Meanwhile Benny was ranting at the cops: "Arrest one of my players! In the middle of an FA Cup Fifth Round tie! You gotta be out of your tiny minds. What's he s'posed to have done, anyway...?"

Luke couldn't hear what the arresting officer then told him. Someone shut the door on the players, who laughed a bit, scratched their heads a bit, drank tea a bit – but said very little indeed. They couldn't really, not with Chopper in the corner. The trainees from the bench looked especially goggle-eyed. Benny had made a good call there: the big-day pressure clearly *was* too much for them.

Five minutes later, the door opened and Terry the Physio nipped in. "So what's going on with the Bill?" asked Gaffer, Dennis, Craig and Narris in unison.

"Don't ask me," shrugged Terry. "I've just been making sure the heat's gone off again next door. In two minutes time, the lights'll go out as well. That should put 'em *right* off their stride. It's what you call home advantage."

Then the door re-opened and a solemn-looking figure – half-man, half-sheep – stepped in, followed by the head boy-in-blue. Both eye-balled Chopper.

"Blow me, Chopper," Benny said, shaking his head. "I'm all for 'ealthy competition between the lads for places in the team. But *this*..."

"What, Boss? What's he done, Boss? Tell us, Boss!" piped several braver players, who were standing close to the policeman with the handcuffs.

Benny just kept shaking his head. "Basically, our makeshift striker had young Frederick here *kidnapped*, just so's he could play in this game himself."

Some sharp intakes of breath, the odd gasp – a pretty muted response really. They'd probably been expecting blood, brutality, Bunsen burners...

"Luckily Luke rumbled it," Benny went on, "and got Frederick out in time."

The other players all cheered at that.

All except Chopper. With a horrible leering smile he began to nod at Benny. "You're just having a laugh," he sneered up from the bench-corner he had made his own for two hundred and sixty-nine consecutive appearances. "It's only *his* poxy word," he nodded at Cool F, "against mine."

"*And* the word of your accomplice, Walter Bates," the policeman cut in, producing a sheaf of notes from his pocket in the style of Agent Veal.

Chopper didn't even blink. Still his venomous gaze burned only on Frederick. "Yeah, but that little runt hasn't pressed charges. He wouldn't *dare*."

Everyone looked Frederick's way. Calmly he stuffed the sherbet bag back in his kagoul pocket and licked his fingers. Then he started to nod – looking from the terrified trainees to Luke to Benny to the honcho with the handcuffs and finally at Chopper. He grinned. "Charges – yeah?" he asked. "*After* the game, right? Let's just give it another forty-five. So Chopper can go out with a bang."

"Dunno about bangs," muttered Chrissie Pick, next to him. "A goal would do."

"Yeah-h-h, now..." Frederick glanced at

Luke, who knew at once what his mate was thinking and gave him the thumbs-up. They had safety in numbers. Half the local constabulary was outside. They were pretty well untouchable.

"Maybe," said Luke, "Chopper's luck in front of goal needs to change. Maybe we can do something to *make* it change."

"Yo!" chimed in Cool Frederick. "You still got that pineapple, Craig?"

A nervous titter passed round the room – followed by an enormous sigh from next door, then a barrage of shouting. "What the heck's that?" asked Benny.

"Just the lights going out over Newcastle United," smiled Terry.

By now Frederick was on his feet – and the pineapple was in his hands. If Chopper had never looked at him homicidally before, he did now. "Let's lay this jinx," suggested Frederick, working the piece of fruit round and round.

"Get up, Chopper," Benny told him firmly (and there wasn't even a whiff of hip-flask on him now). "Get up and bend over for the nice young man."

It took Chopper an age, but he did it. Turning, he leaned forward, gripped a wall-peg in each hand, and braced himself for the impact. Luke looked up at Frederick just before he let the thing go. In spite of all the stick he'd taken from

Chopper, there wasn't a trace of malice on the young super-stopper's face. He wasn't wound up, not steaming, not gagging for revenge. Just ... cool. But that didn't stop him from sending down the kind of delivery to make an England opening bowler's mouth water – smashing into Chopper's beam and shattering the fruit into juicy bite-sized chunks all over the dressing-room floor.

Chopper made no sound. The rest of the players (except the trainees, who were probably going to need counselling after this) couldn't help roaring with glee.

"That'll see you right, Chopper," grinned Benny as the bell went to summon up both teams for Round Two of the tie. "Ten quid says you'll score this half!"

Frederick nodded in agreement. "I'll put ten on him scoring too."

"You're on!" yelled everyone else in the room (except the man with the sticky backside). Even the policeman took the bet. "Him score a goal?" he laughed at Chopper. "You're more likely to find a pile of rocking-horse droppings!"

"Right lads," Benny cried, pulling back the door as the Newcastle players blinked their way past in the bright new light. He lowered his voice to the hoarsest of whispers. "You can do these! Look at 'em! They can't see where they're going! Blind leadin' the blind! But you've got the vision. You've got the power. The force is with you. *Now get out there and light up Ash Acre!"*

Madman was the last one out. "Well it's nice to know you're appreciated," Luke heard him moan as he trudged up the tunnel. "Not one word about me saving the pen! You'd think something more *important* had happened!"

25

Albion hit the ground running after the restart. The penalty miss seemed to have knocked the stuffing out of the visitors. Their midfield was looking droopy, their defenders starting to bawl each other out. As for the Ruud Boy, he was up and down like a yo-yo in the dug-out. And their fans' big inflatable Newcastle Brown bottles were getting saggier by the minute.

"What ... A Waste ... Of Money!"
the Albion fans chanted at Shearer every time he got near the ball (which was never very near, courtesy of Cool F). And when he ballooned a half-chance over the bar after a corner, they struck up even louder with:

"You're Not ... As Good ... As Chopper!"
But Shearer was spending less and less time threatening Madman's goal. Since Luke and Co were winning everything in midfield, he kept dropping deep to try to stop the rot. Naturally Frederick pushed up with him, and soon he started to link smoothly with Luke in setting up

wave after wave of Albion attacks. One of these, in the sixty-eighth minute, was an absolute belter.

First Frederick took a square ball from Dennis, shaped up to play a long cross-field pass to Half-Fat, then suddenly swerved inside Big Duncan Ferguson. He didn't just catch the towering Scot off-balance. Two of his teammates were horribly deceived as well, and Frederick swept past them like a duck on a fairground rifle range (only a lot more elegantly, and without being yellow).

The Albion fans sensed there was something on here. Something tasty. In that weird way that sometimes happens at matches, they *dropped* the decibel level but somehow their new throaty roars sounded *more* frenzied than a full-blast, head-back holler. Frederick slipped the ball to Luke and surged on upfield. Chrissie pulled away to the left, Ruel made a great run to the right – both dragging defenders with them – to create a gaping space for Luke to motor into.

But as Warren Barton came out to close him down, and Robert Lee backtracked to keep tabs on Cool F, Luke's only option for a pass was to Chopper. Which wasn't, of course, an option at all. The Newcastle defence sussed that too. No one was bothering to mark him. In fact they *wanted* Luke to let him have it: he was bound to make a right horlicks of any pass he got. *Light up Ash Acre*... Luke thought. *Play smart football*... So he did.

It had to happen fast. Chopper was standing as still as a brick wall. Good – Chopper had always been your man for walls. Without even looking, Luke flicked the ball past Barton – hard at Chopper's shin. Then he raced on ahead towards goal. If Chopper *had* been a wall, he would probably have reacted quicker. Which was perfect. The ball cannoned off his leg straight into Luke's path – a classic wall pass! Barton made a desperate lunge to stop the ball from getting through but only succeeded in pulling a muscle. Luke didn't even have to break stride before potting the white past Given. *One-one!*

The wheels soon came off the goal celebration (an attempt dreamed up by Madman to reproduce the Starship *Enterprise* in flight) but at least no one got injured. The fans then turned up their support to a deafening Warp Factor Nine and with the game running into its final phase, "There Was Only Going To Be One Winner" – as Kevin Keegan would say.

Newcastle just couldn't get out of their half. Shearer and Ferguson were back on the edge of their own box, helping to repel the bombardment from both Albion wings. Gullit had gone into Dreadlock Overdrive on the line. But even he couldn't call the lads in stripes sloppy. It was just that everyone in blue and white hoops (except Chopper) was well and truly *on it*. Did these boys have their Cup heads on! Cup hair, Cup necks, Cup shoulders and proudly thrust-out Cup chests too!

But the minutes were ticking away. And by some cruel quirk of fate, however many chances Albion created, they kept on falling to Chopper. He could find the right positions, no problem. But unless someone was using him as a human wall he was about as much use as a ref without a whistle. And talking about refs, this one was starting to look at his watch pretty hard.

Luke couldn't be doing with that. He would never get all the way to Tyneside and back for a midweek replay. Rousing himself for one last fling of the dice, he stretched to intercept an ambitious crossfield ball from Newcastle's Speed.

In a flash Frederick was rifle-ranging past him, ready for the one-two. Luke delivered and set off himself. Frederick gave him waitress service back – bypassing three striped shirts. And when Luke then took out two more with another flawless first-time ball, Cool F was almost clean through on goal. Only Charvet stood between him and the keeper, with Barton still limping by the far stick.

"Yeahhh!" came a vicious roar from just

behind Frederick. It was Chopper – trundling towards the penalty spot and hungry for the ball. Charvet, remembering Luke's earlier move, dropped off to cover Chopper but Frederick just ran on. Charvet gave chase but he wasn't going to catch him now. And still Chopper lumbered forwards.

Shay Given came out to narrow the angle, edging the Cool One towards the byline. Frederick dummied to shoot then calmly took it round him. Now he looked up. Straight ahead was an open goal. To his side stood the guy who'd had him trussed up in a boiler room only two hours before. Luke, watching them both from behind, could only gasp. How cool *was* this boy?

Frederick nodded his head, then stroked the most inviting ball imaginable to the ex-con who was about to become a con all over again. It was a gift, a present, something sweet for him to think about while he stewed in the slammer. Barton stuck out a gammy leg but couldn't reach him. Given, still grounded, flung out an arm but not far enough. Chopper was two yards out – and from there, he was deadly.

As the net bulged and he wheeled away, the final whistle went. At the far end 2,000 travelling Geordie faces crumpled in tears. On the South Side up went the enormous pineapple, sprouting blue-and-white dreadlocks instead of leaves. It was uncanny: as if the faithful had *known* Chopper had taken that half-time hit – and made Benny and Cool F a tidy wedge of tenners from their bet.

Luke flew up to dive on Frederick, the real match-winner. So did all the other Albion players (except Chopper) and every Albion fan who could squeeze past the stewards. They'd done it! They'd hit the massive Magpies with the ultimate sucker punch! Now they were in the hat for the Quarter Finals – just them and *seven* other teams! *They were two games away from Wembley!*

But what about Chopper? He was still running. *On* the run, might have been closer. His team-mates watched open-mouthed as he sprinted faster than at any time in his previous two hundred and seventy games. But he wasn't heading for the tunnel. He was steaming on towards the Town End exit, burning off first two policemen, then four, then half a dozen. He was doing a runner!

The crowd loved it. They thought this was another one of Madman's routines.

"There Goes The Chopper!"

they belted out. Even the Geordies stopped crying for a minute and cheered him on. But quickly the police cordoned off the Town End corner. Squealing to a halt, Chopper swung through one hundred and eighty degrees and set off back along the cinder track for the West End – a route that would take him past his team-mates, all frozen in mid-celebration.

A policeman lurched in for a rugby tackle. Like a matador, Chopper danced away. Another stuck out a foot. The mad bull hurdled it with ease. He was past the halfway line now and *accelerating*. Then, as he charged closer to the pile of players, the burly chief steward stepped out of the North Stand to block his way. Chopper hadn't been expecting that. He swayed left as if to career on to the pitch then in mid-stride veered back and left the big guy for dead on the *inside*.

That got the biggest cheer of all.

"Chopp-ah! Chopp-ah...!"

rang around the electrified ground. But the ovation went to Chopper's head. Steaming on, he just couldn't resist looking back and smirking horribly at the steward. That needn't have led to his downfall. But Luke – watching from the base of the human pyramid ten yards away – saw as clear as crystal why it would.

Only one person in the ground was blissfully ignorant of the chase. Only one person – stepping now over the North Stand's low wall – had something other than Chopper Foggon on his mind. Only one person was grinning at Luke and Frederick and waving a wad of fully-amended client forms. And only one person could possibly have worn Raybans on a dark late-afternoon in February.

"Watch it! *Watch it!*" Luke yelled as Vealy took his first step on to the cinder track. But even if he heard, it was too late. Too late for Chopper, after his backwards smirk, to swing the steering wheel. Too late for the agent to skip out of his oncoming headlights. Luke's eyes nearly popped. Two hundred and fifteen pounds of British beef that was definitely not Farm-Assured smacked into the Streak Of Veal with the force of a fruit-stall full of pineapples.

Both men shot into the air. Chopper spiralled up then crashed down half into the wall, half on to the track – where ten pairs of hands and one pair of handcuffs soon had him where they wanted him.

"I'm not at all sure that you're my favourite person in the world!" he mouthed at Cool F as he was led away (or words to that effect). But Frederick wasn't watching. With Luke he'd crossed to where Vealo lay spreadeagled near the corner flag.

Luke caught his breath. The Elastoplastered agent's Raybans had flown off. His eyes weren't focusing. No part of his body moved. Suddenly Luke feared the worst. "D'you think," he stammered to Frederick, "D'you think he's..."

"No *way!*" Frederick replied, nodding at Veal's hand.

It was beginning to twitch. Still it was clutching the client contacts. Then the agent shook his head, got his eyes straight, and smiled up groggily at the two boys he so desperately wanted on his roster. "*Seven* per cent if you record a Cup Final song...?" he tried to ask. "Look, I think I'll have to get back to you on this..." With a dreamier smile, his eyes closed. "Let's do ... hospital food."

The St John's men had him on a stretcher in moments. As they carted him off, Benny Webb picked up his Raybans and plonked them back on his nose. After that, with the jubilant Albion fans singing and dancing their hearts out, he turned to Luke and Frederick – the undisputed stars of his Smart Football Show.

All three silently high-fived each another. Then they joined together to make the most carefully considered and eloquent post-match analysis of all:

"YEEE-AAAA-HHHH!"

Paul Stewart

Football Mad
2-1 up in the inter-school cup final, captain Gary Connell finds the net ... at the wrong end! Now cup glory rests on a tricky replay...

Football Mad 2
Offside!
The inter-school cup is up for grabs again. But Craig won't be playing. He's been dropped – and he's not happy...

Football Mad 3
Hat-trick!
Could it be cup-final number three? Goalkeeper Danny is in trouble. New team coach Mr Carlton has really got it in for him...